The Heretic

William Baer

Southwell Press

for my family and friends

He that is not with me, is against me.

(Matthew 12:30)

I.

CONFESSION

"The auricular manifestation of one's actual sins, committed since Baptism, to a priest, with the intention of obtaining forgiveness and sacramental absolution."

Chapter 1

Beckoning

(Thursday, August 3rd)

I concluded, the Thursday after Pentecost, that there was no God . . .

Full and luminous, the Roman moon was up there somewhere, high above the glittering city on the Tiber, as I raced my Harley FX Night-Train northeast of the Quirinal Palace. I passed Santa Susanna on the left and Porta Pia on the right, then I made a few quick turns to Via Velletri, where I parked my Harley in front of the nightclub near a mess of Vespas. As always, there was a long line of young Romans and eager tourists waiting to get into The Alien, but I walked to the front of the line, nodded at Carlo, and went inside.

As usual, the place was packed and frenzied. I took off my black blackout helmet, weaving easily through the crowd toward the bar at the left of the club's largest dance floor. Beneath my Parenzo black leather, I was wearing a lime green Brioni suit, tapered, unvented, with a light-green Battistoni shirt of Egyptian cotton with mother-of-pearl buttons. Like most of the Romans in The Alien, I took such things quite seriously, fully aware of how much the so-called "continental look" flattered my own appearance, tall, lean, dark-haired, dark-eyed, and trim.

As I slipped through the crowd of hip young Romans and "with-it" expatriates, I nodded to a few friends and acquaintances, but I didn't stop. The Alien, as always, was a bit excessive, with its futuristic high-tech decor, its wildly pulsing multicolored strobes, and its ear-shattering rock music, but I liked it anyway.

At the bar, I nodded at Lorenzo for my usual, and it came immediately.

"My favorite American," the Italian said, with his semi-comprehensible English and his personable smile.

I smiled back, lifted my whiskey sour, and drank half of it straight down. I'm really not much of a drinker, not by a long shot, but I was worn-out from my busy day in Rome, running all around the sweltering city covering the latest political scandal and the subsequent resignation at the Palazzo Madama, and I felt certain that some booze would help me relax. I was right. It did. Almost immediately, the bizarre, space-ageish, way-too-trendy Alien seemed a lot more comfortable. As always, it was a friendly upbeat crowd, and most of the patrons were very well-dressed, even the ones with green hair and neck tattoos. When I finished my drink, I waved for another, then I turned around to face the thumping dance floor and the evening ahead.

I saw her immediately.

Just like, I'm sure, everyone else in the room when they first took a look at the huge dance floor. Certainly all the males. She wore a tight, rather-slinky, red dress that was custom-designed to accentuate the perfectly seductive curves of her youthful exuberant body. She had long, amazingly thickish, black-black hair, that subtly echoed her every movement, glistening in the flashing strobe lights. Even from across the room, her voluptuous red mouth and her dark-Roman eyes were mesmerizing, as was everything else about her. Tall, marvelous, and swaying gracefully and melodically to the music, she was obviously the most beautiful young woman in the city, which was *really* saying something. A dark-eyed Roman goddess that even Praxiteles couldn't have comprehended.

Leaning back against the bar, I sensed that the guy standing next to me was also staring at the Roman girl in the red dress, just like everyone else. Curious, I glanced to my left, and the guy, probably an English or Dutch tourist, shot back:

"*Che bellezza!*"

Which seemed to sum it up in any language.

I nodded my agreement, then the guy took a hit off his beer before staring out at the dance floor once again and settling on the red dress.

When I finished my second and last-for-the-evening whiskey sour, the song ended, the music faded momentarily, and the girl in the red dress left her girlfriends on the dance floor and headed for the bar. Watching her walk, I decided, was just as fascinating as watching her dance. As she came closer, she smiled, lifted up her arms, placed them around my neck, and kissed me on the mouth.

The taste of paradise.

The taste of the one I loved.

I was perfectly content. I could feel her warmth through her slightly-damp dress, and I could feel her heart still thumping from the dance floor.

She wanted more. She gently pulled back her lovely face, smiled again, and spoke in perfect English.

"Dance with me, love."

It was exactly what she always said.

I put my empty glass on the counter and nodded at Lorenzo, who took my motorcycle helmet and stored it beneath the bar.

Then I looked back at Angelina.

"For as long as you want, my love," I said, adding *"Anything* you want."

Which she liked a lot.

She took my hand, and as we started for the dance floor, the *"bellezza"* guy at the bar caught my eye and lifted his beer in appreciation. Why not? I was the luckiest guy in Rome, and no one knew it better than me.

I nodded back.

Three hours later, my love and I were sitting in the Pincio Gardens, high above the eternal city, on the terrace balustrade over Piazza del Popolo. We were sitting on an isolated stone bench within a perfect silence, within the perfect moonlit darkness. It was, of course, the most romantic place in Rome. Small wonder that both Stendhal and Henry James had written about it in their novels, small wonder that everyone in Rome, everyone who happened to be in love, came to Pincian Hill to stroll through the garden park and wander up-and-down its promenades, beneath the dark pines, past the white marble busts of long-forgotten Italian artists and patriots.

She was sleeping.

She was wrapped tightly around me, and her beautiful face was resting on my chest. Gently. The moon was bright and full tonight, just a few days shy of a lunar eclipse, which we were planning to watch together this Saturday on the beaches at Cannes. Tonight, the celestial Queen of the Night was perfectly full, regal, and radiant, shedding her soft tender light over the whole fantastic city and onto the face of my Angelina. Ever since I was a little boy, back on the Maryland coast, I'd had a special fascination and love for the earth-moon, with all its mythologies, and, tonight, I found myself recalling the lovely lyrics of an old Middle Eastern song:

"All young women are stars,
but my beloved is the Moon!"

How true. Angelina and the moon, in their own extraordinary ways, were both perfect.

I smiled at myself and my pleasant romanticisms. I was fully aware that I tended to over-idealize the love of my life, but, then again, why shouldn't I? Shouldn't every young man, if he was *truly* in love, feel exactly the same way? Besides, if anyone deserved it, Angelina did.

Satisfied, I glanced outward, over my adopted city. In the softly diffused moonlight, I could see the slowly winding Tiber, Castel Sant'Angelo, the great dome of St. Peter's, the Pantheon, and the ever-so-white and overly disparaged monument to Victor Emanuel II.

Directly below, I could see the lamplit Piazza and Porta de Popolo, one of the ancient and traditional entrances to the city. Back in 1655, Pope Alexander VII had commissioned Bernini to redecorate the Porta's inside façade for the arrival of the recent Catholic convert, Queen Christina of Sweden. I assume that the great queen must have felt very welcome when she first arrived in the imperial city.

I certainly felt that way when I first arrived in Rome three years ago.

Angelina stirred.

Gently.

Then she held me even tighter, sighing softly, which exhilarated my heart. In fact, everything that Angelina did exhilarated my heart. Unfortunately, her slight readjustment on the bench had left her lovely legs slightly uncovered, and since the night was now carrying a definite chill, I leaned to my left and repositioned my leather jacket to keep her warm. I'll keep her warm forever. I'll protect her always. Then I looked down at her face, and I kissed her forehead. Why was I so fortunate?

I had no idea.

Two summers ago, I pulled my Harley up to Giolitti's over on Via degli Uffici not far from my flat near the Pantheon, and I saw her sitting on a brand-new, bright-green Vespa eating pink ice cream. Probably strawberry. I took off my helmet and spoke casually, instinctively. I was, of course, instantly aware of her astonishing beauty, as she sat there, totally absorbed in her ice cream cone, sitting on her little scooter in a sleek green dress. But what struck me the most, at that exact moment in time, was her extraordinary pleasure and contentment.

"*Quella é una buona idea,*" I said simply, without really thinking about it.

It was just a passing comment, not really intended as a come-on of any kind. It was just something pleasant you might say to someone as you got on the queue to buy some ice cream. But Angelina froze right where she was and looked at me directly, *very* directly, looking me up-and-down. She was, I was aware back then, deliberating about how she should respond to my innocuous comment, or even *if* she should respond at all. But as I'd later learn, she was also thinking about quite a bit more than that, about her whole life, in fact, about whether this might be the pivotal moment in her young life, one that she'd long been anticipating. She was wondering, within her racing whirling mind, whether this random and innocent encounter with a tall American stranger might be, or might not be, crucial to the entire rest of her life.

She decided.

"Try it," she said

She smiled, and she held up her ice cream cone.

I tasted the ice cream. Luscious strawberry. Our eyes met, we smiled, and we fell in love. Actually, I did. Angelina had already done so a few moments earlier. She'd taken one look at the tall stranger in his custom-made leather jacket and his tapered dress pants, and decided, for whatever unfathomable reason, that he was the "one." It was that simple. That was that. From my point of view, her reasons were perfectly inexplicable, and they've always remained so. I was aware, of course, that I was a rather attractive and likeable guy, and I'd had a number of pretty girlfriends in my previous life, but to have this extraordinary young girl, who was just nineteen years old at Giolitti's (five years younger than me), look at me once, just *once*, deliberate for a single moment and decide that she loved me without qualification, always seemed to be nothing short of miraculous.

Even her name was beautiful.

Angelina Parenzo.

She shared an apartment near Trevi Fountain with her cousin, Isabella, not far from where I lived. She was the daughter of Croce Parenzo, who'd emigrated from Fiumicino to lower Manhattan when he was eleven years old, quit high school at sixteen, then married a beautiful American girl from Lavallette at the Jersey shore. Quickly, he built up a leather goods empire with centers in Paris, New York, Milan, Madrid, and, of course, Rome. Angelina, who was born here in the ancient city, with dual citizenship, was their first and only child. She was obviously and admittedly spoiled, but, rather remarkably, it almost never showed up in her personal behavior. She grew up in Manhattan, on the Upper West Side, spending her summers at the family villa in Rome. When she was a junior in high school, business forced her parents to move the family to Rome for two years, which she didn't mind at all. She was, in truth, content anywhere.

Everywhere.

Later, when it was time to graduate, she decided to stay with her Roman friends and go to La Sapienza where she studied the only subject she'd ever had any interest in studying: art and fashion design. The year before we met, she'd opened up Parenzo's, which quickly became one of the most fashionable boutiques on Via Borgognona, specializing in leather clothing, all of which she designed herself. She was charming, creative, loyal, honest, ethical, fun, and for some ridiculous reason in love with a guy named Bryce Sinclair.

Me.

I looked up at the moon again.

Ptolemy believed that the lunar satellite made people unstable and erratic. For the Greeks, the moon was not only the symbol of the beautiful and chaste Artemis, but also of the dark internal subconscious forces that lie within the hearts of every single man and woman, lurking within some kind of mysterious "lunar zone," within the hidden place where all our blackest fears and instincts and impulses ran rampant. Occasionally, the mysterious moon, with its effervescent moonlight, would coax these things to the fore and incite them to manifest themselves. Somehow, the moonlight had the capacity to upset our delicate equilibriums and entice us to indulge our primordial urges, ones that we definitely repressed in the bright revealing lights of the day-star.

Crime and suicides, as often noted, always increase in the moonlight, which also incites insomnia and its agitating companion "anxiety." Some cultures believe that humans can actually be moonstruck, just as they can be sunstruck, and that the condition induces sleepwalking, hallucinations, and other disturbing behaviors. A number of scientists, possibly pseudo-scientists, have even speculated that the powerful tidal pull of the moon, especially the full moon, affects the living waters within our individual cells, increasing our stress, creating psychic disruptions.

Not for me.

The moonlight has always made me calm. Always. Even as a child on the Atlantic coast in Maryland. Every night before going to bed, I'd slip out of the house and sit on the beach, all alone, even in the winters, and relax within the luxuriating silver gleams of the moon. It never failed to give me a sense of equanimity and comfort and resolution. Just like tonight, holding my lovely Angelina, thinking about what she'd said earlier tonight, right here on the bench, before she'd fallen to sleep.

"I think you need to do it soon," she'd decided, as if from nowhere.

"Do what?" I wondered.

"Ask me to marry you, of course," she replied, as if it was perfectly natural, perfectly obvious.

"Then I will," I assured her immediately, perfectly pleased that the time had come.

Then, silently, we thought about it together, separately, in the soft Roman moonlight. I wanted nothing else in the world. Nothing more.

"I want to make love," she said gently.

Which we'd never done.

Which, of course, would have shocked all our chic young friends in Rome, who naturally believed us to be passionate young lovers. Which was even odder since it had absolutely nothing to do with the nominal Catholicism that Angelina had lapsed away from years ago. But there was another reason. When she was twelve years old, she'd made a solemn promise to her father, soon after one of her Italian cousins had gotten pregnant at fifteen in Viterbo and then come to America to abort her baby. That unpleasant, sad, and ugly experience had had a powerful impact on Angelina's young life. A permanent impact. Suddenly, as she stood on the threshold of her own blossoming sexuality, she apprehended the awesome responsibilities of sexual behavior, so she went to her father one night, at their beach house in

Lavallette, and told him exactly what she intended to do. Which was very simple: she would "save it" for marriage.

The decision had nothing to do with her parents. There'd been no prompting whatsoever, but, quite naturally, her father was extremely pleased, even though, within his own pragmatic heart, he probably couldn't fully convince himself that his beautiful daughter would be able to do what she was promising to do. But she had. She would be a virgin on her wedding night, and she had absolutely no regrets about it. None whatsoever. In fact, things had worked out exactly as she'd always felt they were supposed to work out. She'd, rather simply, waited for the "right one" to come along, decided that it was me, and never faltered. But now, finally, she was talking about "making love." It was finally time for me to ask her, to marry her, and to love her forever.

Nothing could be easier.

My stupid pager beeped.

Irritated, I leaned over and looked at the message on the little work pager that I kept attached to my leather belt:

Call 06 69824812 now

Whenever my boss at the *Herald* said "now," he meant *now*, but the nearest phone booth was down on the Piazza del Popolo. Naturally, I didn't want to move, but I knew that I had to.

"I'll be right back, love," I said softly.

Angelina murmured something that was close to an acquiescence, so I carefully disentangled myself and raced down the dark stairs into the piazza.

Fortunately the phone booth was empty, so I quickly dialed the unfamiliar number.

The message was strange to say the least.

"*Quando?*" I asked to reconfirm what I'd just heard.

"Now."

The old man's Italianize English was heavily accented.

I glanced down at my watch.

It was 1:15.

"Now?" I double-checked.

His response was firm, unequivocal.

"Right now."

"*Va bene,*" I responded, then I hung up the phone and raced back up the stone steps to my lover.

Angelina, still sleepy yet definitely curious, was still sitting up on our stone bench.

She was now wearing my leather jacket, waiting patiently.

"Work at this hour?" she asked.

"Not really."

I sat down beside her, still thinking things over, still confused.

She looked at me closely, as if to say, "Well?"

"It was the Vatican."

She looked at me suspiciously.

"Just *what* are you up to, Signor Sinclair?" she asked mischievously.

"Nothing," I assured her, "I've got nothing going on at the Vatican."

So we sat together in the moonlight, within the silence, for a few brief moments.

"Cardinal Visconte," I said out loud. "Do you recognize the name?"

She shrugged.

"I've heard of him before. He's one of the big boys."

"Then why's he calling me?"

"Because you're my secret agent man!" she said with a smile, and I laughed.

No matter how hard I'd tried to disabuse Angelina of that silly notion, she always assumed, given my background over at the embassy and my political work for the *Herald*, that I was aware of a lot more secret stuff than I really was.

I looked into my lover's eyes.

"I hate to leave. I *always* hate to leave you."

"Then do me a favor?"

"Anything," I assured her.

"Kiss me a thousand times before you go."

I laughed again as we came together in the cool and perfect moon-light.

I tasted her lips.

Yes, she was definitely the taste of paradise.

When we finally fell apart, she looked into my eyes with another mischievous smile.

"One," she counted out loud.

Leaving only nine hundred and ninety-nine to go.

I kissed her again.

. . . at least no personal god, no merciful god, and certainly no Catholic god. It was, I can assure you, an extraordinary relief. Release. Comfort. I'd finally found the will to stand up for myself and refuse to further demean myself intellectually. It's hard to describe what a powerful pleasure it was to fully apprehend the truth, to say it out loud in my heart. To fully accept it. All the years of pretension were gone, gone forever. All the interior hypocrisies that had subsumed my entire previous existence had finally come to an end. There would be no more self-deception. The interminable struggle against the perfectly obvious fact of the void of human existence had finally run its natural course.

I suppose it might be hard for the likes of you to comprehend such an intellectual leap, such an intellectual affirmation and admission, but, be assured, I felt, at last, perfectly free and triumphant. I'd finally found the courage, as Russell once put it, to look into the face of the void and accept it for exactly what it is. To accept the unqualified meaninglessness of my own petty little existence. With its total silence. Its godlessness. Its vacuum. From that moment forward, I would never again be consumed by the compulsion to feign or fake a faith in something so ludicrous. To pretend to believe what was patently absurd, patently preposterous. It's true that the great Tertullian once claimed that he believed in Christ because it was "absurd," but, in the end, as he surely knew in his fiery Montanist heart, absurdity demands the full and final acceptance of exactly what absurdity is: the complete and categorical absurdity of ab-solutely everything. Belief, of course, under such circumstances would be totally dishonest, demeaning, and, ironically, absurd.

So, yes, there was a sudden stupendous swell of relief in my life. Of liberation. I felt, in a sense, reborn to the truth. Yet having fully admitted it to myself, I should warn you to be very careful about reaching any unwarranted and foolish conclusions regarding such a simple admission of fact. My decision was made affirmatively, to fully accept the absolute innate truth of the world around us, and it was never, never, in any way, undertaken to escape from the rigors, the demands, or the obligations of the faith. I'm confident that each of you know me well enough to know that I would never take the "easier" path, or that I would never have the slightest desire to mitigate my ascetic mortifications or responsibilities. I'm sure that you'll remember that, quite naturally, by my very nature, I actually prefer more rigorous and tortuous challenges. In fact, that's exactly the path I chose that memorable Thursday after Pentecost. How easy it had been, in the past, to droop into the reassuring arms of holy mother church, effecting all her easily-effected little tasks, dreaming the dream of heavenly paradise. But now, such a facile facility and ease and comfort, along with all its methods and methodologies, were suddenly gone and forfeit forever. I was now proceeding on a far more demanding and exacting path: living faithless in a meaningless world.

But, of course, I was still a priest.

What should I do?

I could leave the church, which many others had done under similar circumstances. It would certainly be easy enough. Write a letter and toss my collar in the fireplace. But I didn't want to. It was really that simple. In truth, I liked the church. Quite a bit, in fact. I admired its complexity, its power, its history, its political intrigue, and, most of all, of course, its unrivalled intellectual stimulation. The Roman Catholic church is, I'm sure we can all agree on this, the most intellectually complex nexus on the face of the earth, in the entire history of the world. Without doubt, it subsumes absolutely everything. It is, *in the truest sense, the "complete" history of the world. Everything else is but a footnote, a reference, or a precedent. It's very easy, of course, for ordinary everyday priests to lose sight of this extraordinary fact, but not for the intellectual. Any human being, with even the slightest education and even the slightest intellectual curiosity, will invariably and naturally be drawn to the Catholic church. It's inevitable. It's inexorable. It's the all-embracing innate fact of human existence. Those who have never immersed themselves in the endless labyrinths of her doctrines, her mysteries, her canons, her hagiographies, her encyclicals, her histories, and all the rest of it, have, as a result, lived nothing but shallow, thoughtless, know-nothing lives. They're intellectual primitives, and they're condemned to stay that way. They have neither knowledge, nor perspective, nor curiosity, nor creativity. The astonishing fact, both unfortunate and undeniable, that, at its very base, it's predicated on a single untruth (Tertullian's "absurdity") changes nothing. Absolutely nothing. All serious men of the mind will eventually subsume themselves in the church. Everything else is frivolous.*

So what should I do?

I certainly couldn't give it up. That was impossible. That was a fate worse than death. And I certainly didn't want to set myself "off to the side" somewhere and snipe at the church like some kind of ineffectual malcontent. No, I wanted to remain right where I was, in the warmth of her bosom, and do whatever it was that I wanted to do.

But what was that?

Actually, Voltaire helped a little bit on that. In general, I've always found the man rather pedestrian, far more posture than brains, but he was definitely right about one thing: religion's not so bad for the peasants because it makes their lives more orderly and comfortable, and not only for them, but for the rest of us as well. Religion discourages their lowbrow drunkenness and childish disobedience, their natural tendencies to riot and vandalize. From the Encyclopedist's point of view, religion was a kind of fascinating parlor game for the intelligentsia. It was like a vast, cosmic, and entertaining game of chess, which is forever sunk in some intractable middle position that was both impossible and undesirable to abandon. I suppose, for clarity's sake, I should make it clear that the analogy's mine, not Voltaire's, but you get the idea. I'm assuming that I can make the safe assumption that all of you play, at least, at some rudimentary level, the game of chess.

Arouet, rather famously, once said "annihilate the church," but if he'd really been able to do so, he would have been left with absolutely nothing to do, and I'm sure he was bright enough to be cognizant of the fact. At any rate, returning to my own situation, it seemed perfectly logical to stay right where I was and continue to "play the game." It would be foolish and detrimental to leave. It would be even more foolish to attempt to destroy it. Which, of course, is always much easier said than done. On the other hand, it would, of course, be most stimulating and gratifying to "modify" it somewhat. Subtly. To somehow mitigate the whole incredible thing. To somehow re-adjust it to my own tastes. To, shall we say, re-make it in my own image. The thought was invigorating!

Exhilarating!

Don't annihilate the thing, make it your own!

Now, as all true intellectuals are cognizant, there's only one war in this world, and that's the war between the world and the Roman Catholic Church. Nothing else matters beyond this all-encompassing conflict that subsumes both life itself and all eternity. So I resolved to spend the rest of my life in an unrelenting assault on holy mother the church, but not attempting to destroy her, but rather intending to re-create her as something completely different and new, something far more appropriate to my own intellectual proclivities.

Of course, as we all know, such a process was already under way. For two millennia. Didn't Augustine back in the Fifth Century concern himself about the "many hidden heretics" lurking within the church's midst? In a way, I suppose, it actually begins with Simon Magus, then the Eastern gnostics, then, most powerfully, Arius and his clever patron Eusebius. But in more recent times, it was most visible and obvious with the so-called modernists. Loisy, Duchesne, Tyrrell, von Hügel, and, of course, Teilhard (who, it must be admitted, hardly seems very modern anymore). Who all tagged along with the so-called "higher critics" and von Harnack and Renan, disabusing the Bible and delimiting Christ. Whatever reservations I had about the whole lot of them, and their obvious failings and limitations, I was quite stimulated by the prospect of following in their general path. In a way, I was determined to complete their work. And what exactly was their work? Nothing less than the de-divinization of Christ. How perfectly extraordinary! I would become, as St. John so aptly put it in his First-century rant about heretics, "a man who dissolves Christ."

I took up my pen, concocted an appropriate pseudonym, and mollified Christ. The first result was my book Le Christ humain. *As intended, and carefully structured, its methodology was subtle and subterfugeous. It feigned a devotion to the teacher-Christ, but gently, gradually, convincingly, pounded away at the illogic of his divinity, while always exalting his humanity in all its undeniable attractiveness. It was a pleasurable exercise. Most pleasurable! An ingeniously crafted balancing act with Christ himself. It was, as I'm sure you'll all remember, very well received, especially in Europe. Nevertheless, the text left me unsatisfied somehow. Yes, the book had appropriately stimulated the intellectuals, who analyzed it ad infinitum, but, let's face it, they're a pretty easy bunch to manipulate. Remember all that silly bluster about Chardin a half-century ago?*

On the other hand, a much more important hand, Le Christ humain *had no real breadth, no broad appeal. It left the thick-headed peasants, who naturally would never bother to read it, still content in their Christological fantasies. Unlike the modernists, I have absolutely no patience for their tried-and-true "trickle down" methodology: infect the theologians, let them invade the seminaries, then engrave their nouveau theologies on the blank-slate little minds of their seminarians. Who, when finally ordained, will suddenly spew forth, spreading their clever little heterodoxies to all the lowbrows sitting in the pews. Well, of course, I knew it worked. The history of the church is replete with countless examples of this kind of subtle and insidious promotion of heresy, but it always left me rather cold. I wasn't planning to live forever, and I was perfectly willing to admit to myself that I wanted a much more immediate gratification.*

So I read over The Human Christ, *with careful detachment and objectivity, and I realized the problem. It was too academic, too mechanical, too precious. There was no real drama, no stunning speculations, no engaging creativity. The book, quite simply, wasn't imaginative enough. It wasn't original enough. In order to affect the masses and jar them out of their torpid complacency, it was absolutely necessary to stimulate their imaginations. This was, fundamentally, the problem with the whole modernist gang, or at least, one of their many problems. They all lacked imagination. Even Chardin, with his silly speculations about "cosmic dust," and "Christ-the-Evoluter," and "divine milieu," and "teleological omegas." That kind of clever intellectual nonsense offered nothing that was dramatically stimulating. In truth, Teilhard was just another subtle heretic, always playing his clever and frivolous parlor games for a narrow audience of fashionable clerics. But I was craving much more than that. Much more. You can always stimulate the intellectuals with a clever play on words and jargony concepts, but you can only enflame the world at large with bold theatrical drama.*

I knew what I had to do, and I knew exactly whom I needed to emulate: the great heresiarchs. So I went back to my library and lived amongst them, all of them, amid those extraordinary speculatives who had, each in his own way, offered up a theological vision so strikingly original and comprehensible that they altered the world forever. I re-read them all, each and every one: Cerinthus, Arius, Macedonius, Pelagius, Nestorius, Mohammed, Berengarius, Constantine of Samosata, Wyclif, and, of course, Luther, who, in the end, spawned twenty-five thousand denominational bastards, "sects of perdition" to cite the Petrus's description, along with an immediate and subsequent 130 years of civil war, massacre, devastation, and ruin.

It was exhilarating.

I positively reveled in my endlessly invigorating re-engagement with the great heresiarchs and all their fantastical schemes and bold manipulations of doctrine. Yet, still, I was somehow dissatisfied. I felt that none of them had gone quite far enough. I wanted to somehow out-heretic the sub-limest of the heretics. Then, on a seemingly obscure summer afternoon, it finally came to me. I was resting in my library, languid in my lingering frustrations, when I glanced up at my bookshelves and noticed an old volume by Borges. Suddenly, instantly, miraculously, instinctively, I re-called his "Tres versiones de Judas," a short quasi-short-story-speculation by the Argentine that I'd once read in my seminary days. The concluding idea of the piece was quite simple, yet more fantastical than anything yet conceived in the relentlessly speculative 2000-year history of Christian heresy.

In the story's first "version," Judas, alone of the apostles, intuits the true redemptive purpose of the Incarnation and decides to become the betrayer of Christ as a "complimentary" sacrifice, as a parallel, as a subsidiary yet heroic act of human degradation and humility.

In the second more theological "version," Judas chooses to do what he does as a kind of ultimate spiritual asceticism, a total denial and mortification of the pleasures of the spirit, which he apprehends are only for God, and for God alone, which leads him to the betrayal and an everlasting embrace of hell.

But it was the third "version," which like the other two are attributed to the fictitious theologian Nils Runeberg, which invariably commanded my attention. It apprehends the fact that the redeeming son of God, in order to effect salvation, needed to demean and humiliate himself as much as humanly possible. Thus the "real" redeemer is not Jesus Christ, but rather Judas Iscariot himself. Thus Judas is God, and God is Judas, the most despised and vilified of all human beings.

These fantastical notions were, of course, just the entertaining and enjoyable speculations of some blinding pedant sitting in his library in Buenos Aires with nothing else to do. It was far too preposterous, far too theologically unsound, to be anything but fiction, but it made me realize the direction I needed to go. It gave me the creative stimulation to move forward, and ironically, this new incentive and innervation eventually led me back to Basilides, whom, by sheer coincidence, Borges had actually mentioned, almost in passing, in the first line of the Spanish text.

I was ready.

I initiated the process by recalling the extraordinary speculations of the Second Century Alexandrine about the role of the "cross-bearer," Simon the Cyrene, in the history of Christ's passion. I was naturally pleased with how comfortably these notions tied in with both the heterodoxies of the Cathars and the arcane history of Rennes-le-Château. Out of it all, I eventually fashioned and created Cyrenianism.

Then I wrote Le Cyrène.

I can still remember the day that I brought the finished manuscript to the printers. I was absolutely buoyant that afternoon as I made my way along the winding, brightly lit, cobblestoned streets. Suddenly, I recollected an old challenge that was once issued by one of our more orthodox professors back in the Pontifical College in Rome. He'd been discussing the heretics that day, the Jovinians, I believe, and he summed up his lecture with a stern warning: "Let he who is smarter than Aquinas cast the first stone." So I thought to myself, walking down the streets with my just-completed manuscript under my arm, "Fine, old man! Here's the first stone!"

At any rate, by now, I'm sure you've all read the book, at least once, even if you'd like to pretend that you "never bothered." You'll remember that it began as a sudden and surprise best-seller in France, swept quickly across Europe, then eventually dropped into that great intellectual void of the Americas. Millions of copies were disseminated, and they're still out there, right now, everywhere, constantly being read and re-read, discussed and disputed, and each and every one of those copies of the book is effectively "dissolving" the Christos. All of Europe, and much of the rest of the world, found itself fascinated by the "could-it-really-be-possible?" mystery of the Cyrenian, and by the equally tantalizing mystery of the book's pseudonymous author. It was, of course, a matter of great personal amusement to hear the various media and curial speculations about who might be the secretive anonymous "Fr. Bernardi Sorel."

From my vantage point, the whole affair was perfect, and perfectly gratifying. The book had appealed across the board, just as I'd intended. There was more than enough clever dogmatic "revisionism" to stimulate the highbrows, and more than enough "story" to fascinate the hoi polloi, while its precisely modulated combination of the two also easily sucked in all those in-between, those pernicious ubiquitous middlebrows. Without a doubt, Le Cyrène *was the greatest personal satisfaction of my entire life.*

As you all sit there, so silent, "dumb" and "dumb" in both senses of the word, you're wondering to yourselves, "But could he really believe such a thing? Could he really believe such a totally preposterous idea?" So I'll answer your unasked question: yes, in a way, I do. Surely, I've made the whole thing up, modifying, intellectualizing, and improving on Basilides. And, yes, it's totally absurd. But, then again, so's everything else, right? So, in the end, why shouldn't I believe it? In truth, it's just as real as anything else that I've ever believed in, as I've wandered alone, reasonably self-sufficient, through the vagaries and illogicalities of this fantastical world in which we're all so briefly trapped. So in response to your never-asked question, the answer is, surprisingly, "yes." I do believe it. I believe it just as much as anything else I believe, or anything else that I've ever believed.

Not that it matters.

Chapter 2

Pontifex Maximus

(Friday, August 4th)

Then, two weeks after the death of my mother, I fornicated for the first time . . .

Forty minutes later, after kissing Angelina *"buona notte"* in the Pincio Gardens, I was walking down the deserted, interminably long corridor of Sale Paoline past the Vatican Library. I had no idea why. Earlier, when I arrived at the Vatican offices, I was told, rather perfunctorily, to follow a somewhat formidable, ever-taciturn Swiss Guard. Immediately, we entered the Vatican Palace at the left of the Basilica, passed beneath the Sistine Chapel, walked through the first-floor galleries, then passed the library. Eventually, we turned left near Atrio dei Quattro Cancelli, before entering the Pinacoteca.

It felt very peculiar to be walking through the immense papal palace and its endless empty galleries in the middle of the night. Everything was motionless, shrouded in darkness. The pure silence of the night was only disrupted by the soft sounds of our careful footsteps reverberating down the long high corridors. On the walls around us, in every room we passed, hung the countless priceless treasures of the civilized world, sitting unlit within the shadows, temporarily unobserved, yet pregnant with discernible yet ineffable aesthetic power.

Eventually, we turned into one of the rooms of the Pinacoteca Gallery, which was partially lit, and I was led to a small wooden bench set before a picture I immediately recognized.

Caravaggio.

A masterpiece.

The guard stopped, then nodded.

"*Uno momento, Signore*," he said with surprising politeness, before turning around and leaving the room. I never bothered to ask the man what was "going on," because I was certain he had no idea. I would have to wait. *Uno momento*, perhaps. Resigned, I sat down on the little bench, which was obviously temporary, placed where it was just for me. Then I looked up at the dead body of Jesus Christ. It made me wary, even edgy. After all, what did the picture mean to me? Except as a kind of undeniable artistic masterpiece? *Who* was that dead man, after all? No doubt, he was a rather extraordinary Jewish preacher, a quasi-Rabbi, a man of profound spiritual depths, of magnetism, but hardly a God. Hardly *the* God. Hardly the supreme being that had supposedly created the heavens and the earth. How could anyone possibly be expected to believe such a thing?

During my three rather extraordinary years in Rome, first as a quick-riser and hot-shot at the American Embassy, before shifting over to a much more exciting and stimulating position at the *Herald*, I'd, rather assiduously, avoided the Vatican. I'd also been avoiding all the other great churches in the ancient city, and I'd been doing so, I now realized for the first time, sitting in the Vatican shadows beneath *The Entombment*, quite unconsciously. Without any intended premeditation. Without *any* awareness of any kind.

It made me rather uncomfortable to finally apprehend it.

But why should I care? What was the big deal?

How does one lose one's faith anyway?

Surely, there are millions of different ways, but the one-time convictions of my youth had simply drifted away, rather gracefully, rather seamlessly, rather painlessly. At the time it was happening, I was barely aware that it was happening. Or that it had finally happened.

Over and done.

I'd been born and raised in the Union's only "Catholic" state, founded by a convert and named for the mother of Christ. I was descended from the Calverts on my mother's side, and my father's father had once served, over fifty years ago, as the US liaison to the Papacy. Although the Sinclairs (the Saint-Clairs) didn't have quite the distinguished Maryland genealogy as the Calverts, they were equally Catholic, being distinguished Highland Scots who'd supported St. Margaret of Scotland; Robert the Bruce; and Mary, Queen of Scots. They were also strong supporters of the Jacobite cause, but, sadly, ended up divided at Culloden. Something we prefer to forget about. At any rate, whatever the distant past, I was raised as Catholic as a Catholic could be Catholic. I was even named for a priest, my grandfather's brother, my father's uncle.

Then I'd fallen away.

Lapsed.

My father believed that everything had gone wrong when I went off to NYU in 1976. My old man wanted his only son to go to St. Thomas More, a newly founded, dead serious, and traditionally orthodox little college in the New Hampshire woods at Merrimack. But at the hyper-engaged age of eighteen, I had no desire to sit around some classroom in the middle of nowhere discussing the *Summa* with a bunch of religion-obsessed kids. No matter how nice they might be. I was young, flush with life, and ready for the real world. Which meant New York City. Where else? But I didn't take off for the city with the intention to behave in counter-productive, foolish, contrary, or reprehensible ways. Actually I had no interest in that kind of useless rebellion. I went to New York to become part of the real world, to be at the dead-center of the where-it's-really-happening world of my generation.

My mother believed that everything had gone wrong when I lost Kimberly, when she dumped me eight years ago. We'd been inseparable since junior year in high school, and we had every intention of marrying after college. The fact that Kim was staying in Maryland to study at nearby St. Mary's, just seventy-five miles east of Ocean City, and that I was planning to head north to the Empire City, didn't faze either one of us in the slightest. *Nothing* would come between us. We were both certain about that, and we were both wrong. Kimberly, despite her fun-loving nature, was, to be honest, more fundamentally serious than I was. As well as much more Catholic. When she realized that I'd become something different from what I'd seemed-to-be before I left for New York, meaning that I was no longer practicing the faith, she called things off. Reluctantly. I was a sophomore at NYU at the time, and, even now, I feel hurt by the memory. Afterwards, I had a few subsequent flings and short-term relationships in the city, and later at Georgetown, but the fact was, and I'm not ashamed to admit it, I'm decidedly monogamous. In the fashion of my parents. I wanted a permanent, regular, always, every-minute-of-the-day kind of love.

And companionship.

Which, of course, I'd now found in Angelina.

My younger sister, Ronnie, believed that everything had gone wrong at Georgetown. She was five years younger than me, always the loving little sister, but on more than one occasion, with our parents listening, she would point out what Bishop Sheen had once said: "If you want your child to lose his faith, send him to a Catholic university." My father, of course, agreed. He'd gone to law school at Georgetown, done well with his practice, estates and wills, and still did endless hours of gratis legal work for the Archdiocese of Baltimore. But he'd never donated a single dime to Georgetown. Like the good bishop, he felt that places like Georgetown and Fordham and Notre Dame had lost sight of their true mission, subsequently secularizing themselves, which was why he was so enthusiastic about the newer, more intellectually rigorous, and more Catholicly-orthodox little colleges like Thomas More, Christendom, and Thomas Aquinas.

So everyone in my family had a theory about the "lapsing" of the oldest child, the only son, the only brother, as they all, unostentatiously, most admirably, maintained their own beliefs and practices. Nevertheless, they were all wrong.

All of them.

There was never one single thing that led to my eventual apostasy, and there was definitely no dramatic inciting event or episode. There was also, curiously enough, no anger, no bitterness, no indignation. There was, in truth, no trauma at all. It simply happened. Gently. Naturally. Over time. In truth, it probably initiated back in Ocean City, and then, over the subsequent years, religion had gradually, almost inexorably, receded from my life. I smoothly slipped into a most comfortable *infidelis*, and I was perfectly pleased with my post-Catholic life. I had no guilts, no sleepless nights, no resentments, no self-recriminations. My parents had raised me well, and I felt that I was still a basically ethical person. I did my best to be decent and caring, and I believed in both charity and compassion, but I never felt the need for any kind of specific faith to motivate me to do the things that I thought were right and just.

But now, right in front of me, was Jesus Christ.

Dead and lifeless.

I looked away. I don't think I can explain why, and my reaction surprised me a bit, but I decided not to worry about it. Not to over-think it. Lying beside me on the bench was a small pamphlet that had obviously been left there for me. I picked it up. It was a brief fact sheet and commentary on the Caravaggio picture, which I read with interest.

The picture had been commissioned by an unknown member of the Vittrice family for their chapel in the Chiesa Nuova in Rome. *The Entombment*, most probably completed in 1604, was immediately and universally acclaimed, considered the masterpiece of Caravaggio's maturity, and it quickly became one of the most highly regarded artistic works of its time. Later, copies were made by such admirers as Rubens, Fragonard, Géricault, and even Cézanne, whose work I never cared for.

Naturally, eventually, the French stole the picture. "Requisitioned" it. In 1797. Then they'd hung it, shamelessly, in the Musée Napoléon in Paris. In time, seemingly motivated by national guilt, the French returned the painting to Rome in 1815, and it was placed right here in the Pinacoteca Gallery. Given its awesome portrayal of post-Crucifixion desolation, the picture is most often compared to the *Pietá* and to Raphael's famous *Deposition* at the Borghese Gallery.

Once again, with a renewed determination, I looked at the picture, at each of its six specific figures. It was truly stunning, dreadful, and overwhelming. The limp dead corpse of Jesus, sharply contrasted against an almost-black background, is gently being deposed in the tomb by St. John and Nicodemus, in the presence of three women: the aging virgin; the Magdalene; and another unspecified, much younger woman. Everything about the scene is dramatic, monumental, classically formulated, and saturate with pathos. The limp, left arm of Christ's corpse is particularly affecting, as is his left hand and his dead face. It seems the very portrait of death itself, and it's terrible to look at.

There's no place to hide.

Standing above the dead Nazarene, higher than the other leaning figures, the Magdalene stands with her arms emphatically outstretched to the heavens. What exactly *is* the essence of the terribly tragic expression on her face? Is it "acquiescence" as the pamphlet suggests? Or is it fear or supplication or execration? Or maybe a kind of stunned incomprehensibility? It's hard to know for sure, but whatever its specificity, there was no doubt about her devastating grief, her helplessness, her tribulation.

Only a tragic genius like Caravaggio could have found the means to express such complexity of depthless cosmic grief. The artist's whole life was a total mess, and his troubles, rather than dissipating with maturity had actually accelerated. Why, I wondered, did such a supremely gifted artist feel it necessary to behave as he did? With his endless brawling, his pre-meditated assaults, his baiting insults, and his stretches in prison. Who could fathom why the man was so disturbed, irascible, and malcontent? And yet, maybe all of it was necessary, so that he could somehow apprehend the catastrophic grief of the internment of Jesus Christ? Maybe it was the only way to properly prepare himself to paint the wracked and wretched face of Nicodemus, holding the corpse of his Christ, gazing out at the viewer, flush with sorrow, and crushed with all the grief of all the history of all the world.

Footsteps.

Relieved, I looked away from the picture, rose from my bench, and saw Luca Cardinal Visconte standing before me.

Tall, lean, imposing, austere, maybe sixty-five.

I leaned over and kissed his ring.

He was unimpressed.

"Are you a practicing Catholic?" he asked, with exquisite English, apparently knowing the answer.

"I'm not," I admitted, feeling a bit foolish, but the cardinal was obviously unconcerned about my feelings.

"Be seated," he said.

I did as I was told.

For a brief moment, Visconte glanced up at the Caravaggio. He seemed totally absorbed, cut-off from everything around him. It was as though I didn't exist. The old man's face, generally expressionless, was now a completely incomprehensible blank. Nothing was visible. Nothing was revealed. Nothing at all.

Nothing was said.

I sat there like an idiot. Finally, abruptly, he looked away, sat down beside me, and rather routinely opened up a thin file he was carrying.

"Are your parents still alive?"

"Yes."

"Your sister?"

"Yes, she's engaged."

There was no response. None.

"Do they practice?" he asked.

"Yes."

The old man made a careful note in his file with a black fountain pen.

"Is Ocean City a resort?" he asked rather incongruously.

"Yes."

"Like what?"

I had no idea what he meant.

"Like Las Vegas?" he suggested.

I was tempted to smile, but I wisely decided against it.

"Not really, it's a beach resort on the Atlantic coast of Maryland. People go there to swim, go fishing, go boating, and go to the amusement parks. The only gambling takes place at Ocean Downs Racetrack which is about four miles west of the island."

He nodded, as if his question had been adequately answered.

"Harness racing," I clarified for no apparent reason.

"Did you work at the resort hotels?" he continued.

"No, my parents didn't approve of the idea, so I worked at the Life-Saving Station Museum while I was still in high school."

The cardinal seemed confused, and I was pleased to see that the man could actually express a discernible state of mind.

"It's a restored life-saving station from 1891," I explained. "It's quite popular with the tourists. It's got old-fashioned life-saving equipment and various exhibits about everything from hurricanes to mermaids."

The last word was unclear to the Italian cardinal.

"Mermaids?"

"Yes, the mythological creatures."

"Ahh," said the old man, thinking whatever he might have been thinking.

I took advantage of the momentary pause.

"I do wonder, Your Excellency, if I could ask why I'm here?"

But the old man had no interest in my petty curiosities.

"Forbearance," he said rather coldly, "is a virtue, young man." Then added, "In *all* cultures."

I had no idea what the cardinal meant, except that, without a doubt, it was intended to put me in my place. Maybe it meant that even the heathens and infidels of this world, like me, generally recognized the value of patience. But I didn't allow myself to take offense. I'd been trained by profession to both wait and listen, so I did so.

"You studied journalism at New York University, then international diplomacy at Georgetown?" he continued, as if there'd been no interruption.

"That's correct."

"Do you have Italian blood?"

Which seemed a ridiculous question to ask.

"No," I said with appropriate forbearance.

"Have you had extensive contact with the Jesuits?"

"Nothing exceptional, just a few teachers at Georgetown."

Even though there was nothing discernible on the old man's face, I detected a sense of relief.

He'd finally been pleased.

"Very good," he said.

Then he stood up abruptly.

I was astonished that everything was over so suddenly. Totally confused, I stood up as well.

"A few moments," the cardinal explained, without explanation. Then he walked away, vanishing into the Vatican shadows.

Alone, once again, I sat down on my little wooden bench, determined to wait as patiently as I could for the cardinal's return.

Initially, I tried to avoid the Caravaggio, but it was impossible. The thing was as awesome as it was irresistible. It lured me in. Rather easily. Once again, I studied the faces, the one now dead, and the others stunned by his death, ending up staring at the shadowed face of St. John, the master's beloved. Then, as if from nowhere, it suddenly came back to me, and I remembered Bruckner. Of course! *That's* why I was here.

About two years ago, when I'd first signed on with the *Herald*, I covered a story about Maurice Augustus Bruckner, a well-known Catholic theologian who'd begun to question the authenticity of the fourth Gospel and was publicly reprimanded by the Vatican. There was no question in anyone's mind that the censure came directly from the top, from the pope himself, so it created a titillating bit of controversy at the time. To make things worse, and much more interesting, Bruckner had also published a little monograph that took a much-too-lenient view of suicide. So there I was, brand-new at the *Herald*, having no idea what to expect, and they sent me off to have a talk with a "heretic."

I was quite surprised by what I found. Bruckner was hardly some rabid, bitter, lay pedant sniping at the edges of the magisterium. He was, on the contrary, a very charming, funny, and personable old guy, who was not in the least bit concerned about what he referred to, always with a smile, as his "papal condemnation." Oddly enough, he was quite sympathetic to the Papacy's position.

"Look," he'd told me back then, "the church has tremendous responsibility. It has to do what it has to do. It's the way things work. Everything needs time."

"But what if you're excommunicated?" I wondered.

"I don't think it'll come to that," he said with a shrug, completely unfazed.

Later, over lunch at an outdoor café on Piazza San Cosimato, I got the old man talking about the suicide business.

"Well, I guess," he began rather reasonably, "it depends on the specific case. After all, Marcus Aurelius, the so-called 'pagan saint,' felt it was appropriate, even noble, under certain circumstances. Is it wrong, I wonder, if incurables, the terminally-suffering, are spared their pain? Who's to say? Who's to judge? Personally, I suspect that God would be highly sympathetic. What do *you* think, young man?"

Despite my misgivings, I was careful and evasive. I didn't want to get sucked in, so I played the role of the objective reporter, and Bruckner didn't seem to mind. We got along very well. In the end, I covered the reprimand flap in the *Herald* with two highly favorable pieces on the dissident theologian. Then, about two weeks later, Bruckner was dead. He'd committed suicide in his little apartment in Trastevere. According to the doctors, he had no life-threatening illnesses, and since his death wasn't a sexy story like his brazen dissidence, it got very little notice in most of the newspapers. Mostly perfunctory obituary notices. At the time, I didn't know what to make of it, and my relentless schedule at the paper and my blossoming relationship with Angelina kept me from giving it too much thought.

Maybe, for some as-yet-unfathomable reason, it was because of my involvement with the Bruckner case that I'd been called to the Vatican in the middle of the Roman night.

It was the best I could come up with.

Visconte was back. I could hear his footsteps approaching, so I stood up, turned around, and saw Angelo Farenti coming towards me dressed in his papal whites.

I was stunned, but I did my best to maintain my composure, which wasn't that hard to do since the gentle Milanese pope had exactly that kind of reassuring effect on people. Whether it was inside the confessional, before papal audiences, or engaged with the crowds of millions who swarmed to see him on his disparate trips abroad. He had a kind, pleasant, rather cherubic face. Years ago, when he'd been the bishop of Milan, he'd developed a reputation as a "priest for the people," which was true, and which had remained true throughout his papacy. He might be tough on dissidents, but his piety and his remarkable charity were obvious to everyone.

I was now standing in the presence of the most famous most beloved man on the face of the earth. One whom many believed to be a "living" saint.

"Mr. Sinclair?" he said softly, with a pleasing Milanese accent, smiling warmly.

I nodded and smiled as well. Then I leaned over and kissed the ring of the Pontifex Maximus.

When I was finished, the aging pope looked carefully and directly into my eyes. It was the middle of the Roman night, something was up, and he wasn't about to waste any time.

"Your uncle is dying," he said simply, gently.

Once again, I was completely stunned. I had no idea that my uncle was sick.

"He'd like you to come," the pope explained.

"Of course," I said, still in shock, still thinking that it was impossible that my uncle, who always seemed so indestructible, could actually be dying somewhere.

"Why didn't he contact me directly?" I wondered.

"Because he wasn't sure that you'd come," he said, honestly, sympathetically.

I understood. For years I'd been avoiding my uncle, and we both knew why. When your faith evaporates, it's rather awkward having an uncle who's an internationally renowned orthodox priest.

"He was also worried that you might delay," the old Pontiff added.

Maybe he was right. Given that I was scheduled to vacation in France this weekend with Angelina, I probably would have delayed the trip to Portugal until Monday or Tuesday.

I nodded, saying nothing.

"There's no time for delay," the pope assured me, and I clearly understood the gravity of the situation.

The pope handed me an envelope.

"Have a safe trip, young man," he said, with remarkable sincerity, "and tell Father that he's in my thoughts."

Then, having accomplished what was necessary, the old pope glanced up at the Caravaggio. For a few moments, he seemed visibly staggered by the weight of Christ's terrible sacrifice and death. Immediately, I understood why we'd met *right here*, of all the other places in the endless labyrinths of the Vatican palaces. I also understood why the little bench had been placed here. It wasn't for me. It was for the Vicar of Christ, the Bishop of Rome, who, in the midst of his long interminable nights, his wearying work, his likely insomnias, would find his way to the eerie silence of the deserted Pinacoteca, to stare at his God, suspended between the Passion and the Resurrection.

To reaffirm himself.

The pope turned back to me.

Gently, he lifted up his hands and placed them over my head, crossing my forehead with his right thumb.

"God bless you and keep you."

Then he turned around and walked away. Slowly, deliberately, he was enveloped within black Vatican shadows.

When he was gone, I opened the envelope. It contained a plane ticket to Lisbon and a tiny voice-recorder with a four-word note:

Tape his final message.

Which seemed rather peculiar.

Then I looked more closely at the ticket. Then at my watch. My flight was leaving from Fiumicino in fifty minutes!

Unthinkingly, I whispered to myself, realizing, even as I said it, that I probably shouldn't be saying such a thing, even in a whisper, within the sacred confines of the Vatican:

"Damn!"

. . . which I suppose was more than coincidental, but certainly not premeditated. There was never any conscious strategy on my part to wait until after her death for the consummation of my sexual desires. I'm equally certain that what happened (so naturally) wasn't some kind of desperate or impulsive repercussion of her passing. Yet I do believe, after the fact, of course, that I probably somehow suspected, deep in my heart, that if I'd broken my vow of chastity earlier, my mother might have intuitively suspected what I'd done. Despite the fact that she never had the slightest suspicions about my dissipated faith, which was exactly what I preferred.

As a matter of fact, I always took the greatest satisfaction in the unabashed pride my mother took in her scholarly son. Her "theologian." Her "genius priest." Her "defender of the faith." So I never dropped my guard. Why should I? Why shouldn't I let her enjoy her little fantasies? I can still remember, quite clearly, one night in particular, when she asked me about something that was disturbing her quite a bit. It was one of Küng's rather pedestrian and unoriginal notions demeaning the divinity of Christ. So I did my best to ease her troubled mind. With both precision and clarity, I explicated away, rather crushingly, I might add, the hubristic pretensions of the stuffy Swiss heretic, even though, of course, I was really quite sympathetic with his general point of view. As a result, my mother was completely gratified and relieved. She reveled in my feigned orthodoxy that night, and I enjoyed giving her the pleasure. It was quite an interesting diversion to play the devil's advocate on behalf of the divineless Jesus Christ.

I would presume that you're all sitting there thinking that I deceived my mother, that I manipulated my mother, and that I patronized my mother. Well, yes, you're correct. All of those things are exactly true. The woman preferred to live her small inconsequential life within the confines of her Catholic fantasy world, and I not only allowed her that comfort, but I encouraged it and even indulged it. I presume that Voltaire would have done the same thing, and, if not, if the man couldn't have given his own mother such an effortless consolation, then the hell with him anyway.

Right?

As for the sex, I was quite surprised just how easy it was. Her name was Geneviève, and she was remarkably beautiful, as well as stupid and willing. She was an unattached, twenty-two-year-old who worked at a local bakery, keeping a small apartment by herself at the edge of the parish. She attended Mass every Sunday morning at seven a.m., sitting in the third row on the left-side of the nave. Not long before things happened, she'd dumped yet another in a long line of inadequate and boorish boyfriends, and I suppose she was ready for something a bit different. Something a bit out of the ordinary. Actually, to be perfectly honest, I started things off rather circumspect, fully expecting a long and carefully plotted pursuit, but she capitulated immediately, willingly, and completely.

Would you like to hear about the first night?

I'm sure you would!

It was in the rectory. In my personal quarters, right beneath my favorite wooden crucifix, which was carved at Port-Royal back in the Seventeenth Century. Without the slightest hesitation, she came up to my room. Immediately. Without compunction. There was absolutely no fear of discovery since we were all alone in the small house. At first, we talked rather comfortably about various kinds of nonsense: Jean Gabin in Pépé-le-Moko, *her first boyfriend, the Magdalene (appropriately enough), even her favorite pastries. I played some Edith Piaf, and we drank some delicious Port. Very quickly, we were both feeling the effects of the wine. Feeling quite comfortable with each other. I had every reason to believe that she was ready-and-willing, and when she asked, "Is there anything I can do for you, Father?" I decided to go for broke, saying, "Yes, why not take off your clothes and lie down beside me?" Which she did, without hesitation, as I watched in amazement, stunned by her shamelessness and her marvelous naked beauty.*

It was that easy.

We hadn't even kissed each other before that night.

Now I must admit, I did wonder at the time, although the Port certainly helped to assuage my concerns, if I'd be able to properly "perform" under the circumstances, having been, until that night, celibate for my entire previous life. But there was no problem.

No problem at all.

Afterwards, I assuaged her easily assuageable conscience. She seemed more concerned about how it might affect my pastoral duties, than with the rather remarkable fact that she'd just whored herself with someone she barely knew. So I fed her all the typical lies and clichés that I'm sure all of the fallen clerics have been offering up to their co-fornicators for the past two thousand years, and she was more than eager to believe the lies and the rationalizations, and that was the end of that.

So we did it again.

I must say, I reveled in the sex. Much more than I'd anticipated. The hot intimate physicality of the sex was far more exquisite than I could have imagined. Up until that night, of course, I'd submitted my life, exclusively, to intellectual sensation and stimulation. But the taste and the touch and the heat of a willing woman, not to mention her exceptional beauty of form and face, with her bright green eyes and her long dark hair was an exhilarating maelstrom of sensation that still remains, in memory, quite indescribable.

I would highly recommend, my dear silly eunuchs, that you both try it some time.

At any rate, over the next few months, everything was perfect. We were perfectly content and perfectly discreet. We saw each other almost every day, and we took long walks on the local hillpaths and down by the beach. On several occasions, I put away my collar, packed my casuals, and we flew off to the Swiss Alps or Majorca or the Costa del Sola for extended weekends together. My time was quite flexible, and my superiors were both naive and disinterested. I felt perfectly satisfied with everything, and it was obvious that Geneviève felt exactly the same way.

I must admit, I was a bit surprised by my own rather uncompromising loyalty. I was fully satisfied with Geneviève, and with Geneviève alone. Opening the rapacious floodgates of my repressed sexuality had not, to my astonishment, incited an interest in other lovers. Geneviève was, in her way, perfect and perfectly satisfying.

Then, of course, she got pregnant.

I'm still not exactly sure if, deep within her heart, she actually wanted it to happen. Maybe even allowed it to happen. In order to force me to do something dramatic. Like abandoning the priesthood. Just for her! For love! How theatrical! How utterly romantic! But, of course, I had, as she quickly learned, absolutely no interest in leaving the priesthood. The fundamental fact of my priesthood, regardless of what I believed (or didn't believe) of the faith itself, was the single most significant and extraordinary aspect of my life, and I certainly wasn't about to give it up for some foolish young woman. A foolish young woman who'd, in all honesty, conducted herself like a common whore.

When I told her to abort the little bastard, she fell oddly silent. She actually seemed hurt and confused and numb, so I did my best to try and comfort her. To make things easy for her. I even promised to take her to the clinic when the time came. I told her that I'd arrange everything. That I'd pay for everything. That I'd make it all up to her. Etc. Etc. But she sat there like an insensate moron, totally unresponsive, crushed and silent. Nevertheless, I kept my calm. I was convinced that things would eventually blow over in time. That she'd finally do the only thing possible under the circumstances. But it never happened. She refused, she argued, she procrastinated, she tuned me out, and, all the while, I was doing my best not to lose my temper. I cajoled, I sympathized, and I gradually turned up the pressure. Then, one day, she suddenly vanished. For a long weekend. Naturally, I wondered what she was up to. Had she gone to the bishop? Had she gone to the press?

Surprisingly, I was quite serene about the entire business. I shrugged my shoulders and said, in effect, "If a scandal ensues, then it ensues." My mother was dead, and even though I preferred not to disturb my comfortable little existence, I had to admit to myself that the thought of a scintillating scandal was quite intriguing, even perversely appealing. It would certainly be very interesting.

It didn't happen.

Geneviève had gone off by herself, to some low-rent clinic somewhere, and had the baby killed. Then she came back and told me exactly what she'd done, like the half-dead survivor of some catastrophic ship-wreck. Then she left. Forever. Surprisingly, there was no dramatic scene. No histrionics. Just a pathetic broken-down young woman telling her priest-lover-companion that she was moving away to "start her life all over again." At first, I tried to dissuade her, but then I let her go. It was the last I ever saw her.

In the immediate aftermath, I was quite amazed by how much I missed her. I actually felt physically numb and depressed for about a week, but, in time, it all passed. Eventually, I was able to admit to myself what I'd always known. That it wasn't really love. It was, of course, very nice to think about such a thing lying next to Geneviève in the darkness of the high Swiss Alps, but underneath it all, I really had no interest in that kind of emotional commitment. I'd always lived my life by the Basilidian maxim, "Know others, but let no one know you." In fact, I'd lived my life that way long before I'd ever encountered Basilides. In truth, I never felt either the need or the desire for what others refer to as a giving or reciprocal or complimentary love, and I had no illusions about my relationship with Geneviève.

But I did miss her.

I missed her companionship. I missed her lovely body. I missed her heated sensual responses to my touch. I missed her complete and utter subservience, which bordered on a kind of abject adoration.

Most of all, I missed the sex.

Cognizant of this rather significant fact, and not inclined to pretend that I was something I wasn't, I soon turned to prostitutes. I discovered that I liked them very much. They were excellent, in fact. They were lovely, discreet, and talented, and there was absolutely no obligation of any kind. As for the money, that was never a problem. As a matter of fact, as my political star had begun to rise in European theological circles, I started having more and more access to various university and seminary accounts. Soon I began to embezzle. Little bits here, little bits there. It was absurdly easy, and, over time, it added up quite nicely. It funded my whores, my Alfa Romeo, and, eventually, my beachhouse on the Côte d'Azur, where I would watch the blue Mediterranean, read theologies, and consume endless streams of delicious skillful prostitutes.

As for Geneviève, she, of course, became exactly the cliché that I'm sure you're all anticipating. She committed suicide in some hovel in Salzburg two months after she'd set off to "start her life all over again." I suppose it will shock each of you, in your various ways, to hear me admit that I had absolutely no remorse. But it's the honest truth. I didn't. I did, of course, have a certain sense of sadness, but, in general, I'm inclined to think that the dead are, generally speaking, far better off dead than we usually assume. For many people, maybe even for most people, the black nothingness of the grave is far more satisfactory and desirable than the day-to-day crap of their daily lives. So if Geneviève came to feel that way, as she obviously had, then I suppose everything was for the best. We all die, right? She just happened to die younger than most, at the age of twenty-two.

So what?

In truth, whether you believe it or not, I wished her the best, both in life and in death. I still remember her fondly, and I think of her sometimes, and I remain grateful for the sex. But I definitely have no remorse, and I never will. We both made our choices, and it was good for a while. Eventually I moved far beyond the likes of her, and her petty demands, and her sex-with-repercussions. All of that now remains in the far-distance past. Never again would I have sex with someone who might desire to be my friend. From now on, sex itself became my friend.

Yes, sex became a very close companion, a rather extraordinary companion, but it never *became the primary fact of my existence or my obsessions. My fundamental impulses never changed. No matter how stimulating the flesh might be, it could never, never, ever hope to aspire to the sublime ecstasies of the intellect. Not by a long shot. In the end, there's absolutely no comparison whatsoever.*

On the other hand, I don't want to mislead you. I don't want to appear too dismissive of my subsequent interest in the varieties of sexual stimulation. Sex proved to be quite a delightful diversion. An amusement. A delicacy. In time, I gradually took up many of the usual quirks and perversions, becoming a bit of a connoisseur of all the various things a woman can do for a man. For a brief period, I even spiced-up the whole business with some rather innovative "sacrilege sex," which I won't describe in detail, given the closed-minded nature of my audience this afternoon. But I will admit, during another brief period, that I actually engaged in various black-rite-Satanic-sex-stuff, although, in the end, I found it essentially dissatisfying. It was too formulaic, too unimaginative. Completely lacking in spontaneity. Besides, it seemed to me that Satan was just as unreliable as Christ.

Nevertheless, I'll say this in Satan's behalf: at least he's for real. Every single religion and every single culture in the history of the world recognizes the daemon, but the good Lord Jesus Christ is only recognized by the one, holy, Catholic, and apostolic religion, and, of course, to varying extents, by its multifarious and ever-squabbling pathetic offshoots.

Chapter 3

Fatima

(Friday, August 4th)

I became a priest for the same reason that a psychiatrist becomes a psychiatrist . . .

The 737 flew effortlessly through the last of the lingering darkness.

Somewhere over southern Spain.

Earlier at the airport, I'd called my boss Jack Gerston at his home and woke him up. He took it in stride. He was a crack-of-dawn type, although not quite this early. Jack had survived several decades of the newspaper wars in New York City, but he was actually a very considerate and reasonable man. These days, as he was closing in on retirement, he seemed perfectly content to run the *Herald's* little outpost in Rome, covering the big Italian stories for the English-language daily that was read by almost every American tourist as well as most of the expatriates. Even though he ran a tight, efficient, professional office, Jack also understood the realities of personal problems and family emergencies.

I told him what was going on.

It was clear to both of us that whoever was working the switchboard at the office tonight had forwarded Visconte's message to my pager.

"I'm sorry to hear about it, Bryce," he said, referring to my uncle.

"I'll try to get back late tonight," I said, "but if I get caught up in Portugal, can I have Monday off?"

Even though I hadn't slept yet, I was still capable of planning ahead.

"Sure, no problem," he assured me. "See you on Tuesday."

That was that.

I was trying to be realistic. Yes, I wanted to visit my uncle, to represent the family, even to make peace with the old man. But I also knew that my uncle might linger for days, maybe even weeks, and I had no intention of staying at the old priest's bedside until the very end. I also knew that my uncle wouldn't expect me to stay for more than a day or two, so I still had hope that I could somehow salvage the weekend with Angelina. I didn't know if it was possible, but I was still trying to leave things open.

"We'll be fine this weekend, Bryce," Jack added.

I knew it was true, and I greatly appreciated his kindness. If anything new broke on the Gaetano resignation/scandal, my buddy, Eddie Watts, could handle it. Roman politics was surely the most complicated and frustrating politics in the world, which was why I found it so intriguing in the first place, but the Gaetano affair was really quite simple. The senator had misappropriated funds, everyone knew it, and he was willing to resign. It was perfectly mundane by Roman standards.

I was very fortunate to have a boss like Jack and a work-buddy like Eddie. Not to mention, such an endlessly fascinating job. After a tedious year of sucking-up to unimportant, usually self-important, guests at the American Embassy, I'd jumped at the chance when the job at the *Herald* popped up. I made a few quick calls, lined up an interview, and got the job. All on the same day. Later that evening, when I left the diplomatic enclave forever, I immediately re-immersed myself in the Roman life that I loved so much. It was incredibly exciting. Incredibly exhilarating. Between Angelina and the *Herald*, I was living the perfect *la dolce vita*, and I knew it, and I was grateful every minute of the day.

I was also grateful, at the moment, for the Vatican's first-class ticket, even though I was unable to sleep. I was planning to call Angelina as soon as we landed in Lisbon, hopefully at 7:15 Roman time, while she was still dressing. In between her wake-up shower and 8:15, when she left her flat every weekday morning for a pre-work breakfast at Bellagio's.

I tried to distract myself, thinking how strange it was that I was flying to Lisbon. If my uncle hadn't been such an exemplary man, I wouldn't be flying to distant Portugal, which is where the conspiratorial progressives had finally managed to exile the formidable Dominican. But the old man didn't seem to mind that much. He loved Portugal. He loved everything about it, in fact, and he'd thrived there.

Actually, he was the kind of man who could have thrived anywhere.

I knew him well, my father's uncle, especially when I was a young boy in Maryland. In truth, I have nothing but fond memories of the man. But ever since Georgetown and my irreparable break from the church, I'd been avoiding the old priest, and now I was feeling guilty about it. He was a truly exceptional man, in all kinds of ways, and from what my father and my grandfather had told me, he'd *always* been that way.

Even sixty years ago, when he was a young boy growing up in Ocean City, it was clear to everyone around him that the priest-to-be was oddly prodigious. For starters, he was flukishly brilliant. Yes, the Sinclair family tree has its fair share of bright and capable people, such as my grandfather, Edward Sinclair, who was a highly respected constitutional lawyer before serving, at his own preference, as a high-level diplomat in Rome. But it was Bryce David Sinclair, my grandfather's younger brother, who was the obvious and unprecedented family genius, who did everything rather effortlessly. Math, languages, sciences, everything. Supposedly, he'd read the entire *Summa* by the age of fifteen! Even more amazing, he'd apparently retained all of it with a kind of photographic clarity. He was so bright as a boy that the family really didn't know what to do with him.

The problem was further exacerbated by two other remarkable aspects of his personality: his apparent normalcy and his unusual piety. On the surface, he was a charmingly personable little boy, not much different from the other kids his age. He loved sports, he had many friends, and he was unusually generous. But he was also devoutly religious. He had a natural and disarmingly cheerful piety about him at all times, which was never off-putting or ostentatious. He was regularly at church, and he developed, on his own, a rigorous prayer life, becoming a model for the entire family.

What's to be done with such an unlikely but likeable young boy?

No one knew, except the boy himself. Apparently, he'd always known. He'd become a priest. And just like Aquinas, he wanted to be a Dominican. Which, in time, he did. When the order finally realized exactly what they had in their midst, they sent him to the Pontifical College in Rome, and he'd spent the entire rest of his life in Europe, visiting his family in Maryland whenever he could get away.

Rising rapidly in Roman theological circles, he was soon teaching at the college. Then, almost immediately, he was brought into the Vatican itself. Even though his star was ascending, the curia felt that he needed pastoral work to round out his overall education, so they sent him to a small parish in Nazaré, Portugal, a beautiful coastal town on the Atlantic, where he served his flock and was much beloved for about two years. When the Vatican brought him back to Rome, he, once again, rose quickly through the corridors of power, eventually working for the Congregation of the Faith and writing a number of highly significant books and treatises. The first was a popular devotional book about the Holy Spirit, *Come Holy Ghost*, followed by his ground-breaking academic treatise on the Cathars, *The Heresy from Albigensum*. Numerous other books followed, all rigorously orthodox, including a biography of St. Dominic, a devotional book about angels, and two more scholarly works on the Manicheans and the *Syllabus* of Pope Pius IX.

Eventually, he was universally recognized as an implacable antagonist of the clerical progressives who were gradually expanding their power within the curia. Unable to challenge him on intellectual grounds and unable to uncover anything scandalous in his life, they decided their only recourse was marginalization. Out of sight. Hopefully, out of mind. So they pulled some strings, bullied a few powerful Dominicans, and got him shipped back to Portugal where he was designated Distinguished Professor of Sacred Theology at the University of Coimbra, the country's ancient university. But he didn't seem to mind. He thrived in the isolation of lovely Coimbra on the famous Mondego River. He was enormously popular, considered a saint by many, and he continued publishing books (one on the Gnostics and one on Pope Leo's *Humanum Genus*). There were even rumors floating back to his family in Maryland that he'd become a close confidant and friend of Lúcia dos Santos of Fatima, now Sister Lúcia Maria of the Immaculate Heart. Over the past ten years, at least two different popes had specifically arranged private visits with the aging priest during their trips to Portugal.

Then, three years ago, he suffered a minor stoke. When he retired from his academic position, he secured permission to move to Fatima permanently. It was perfectly fitting that such a man should live out his life in one of the holiest places on the face of the earth. From that point on, from everything my family has told me, the old priest made a full recovery and was greatly enjoying his life in the Ribatejo.

As always, he stayed in close touch with his family back home, writing letters, calling from Europe, and visiting whenever he could arrange it. As for me, I remember my uncle, my namesake, for whom I was named, extremely well. As a young boy in Maryland, I always looked forward to the special visits of my Uncle-Father from distant

Europe. He seemed so marvelously vigorous and full of life. He was always ready for adventure, quick to laugh, and fun to be with. I treasured our times together. My uncle, always in his blacks and collar, would take me horseback riding, or trips to the amusement park, or fishing in Sinepuxent Bay. For the latter, we'd rise before sunrise, catch a few fish, then talk about everything under the rising sun. Especially baseball, which the old man still followed religiously from far-off Europe.

Always as a Baltimore Orioles fanatic.

I especially remember one sunny morning on the calm Sinepuxent, when I was probably eight or nine, when I asked a silly schoolboy's question about miracles.

"Do you *really* believe in miracles?"

"Of course, I do," he replied good-naturedly, "*all* Catholics believe in miracles."

I was hoping for more, and the old man knew it.

"Look, Bryce, everything in this world is a miracle," he explained, spreading his arms in front of him to the blue waters and the bluer sky. "Did you ever think about that before?"

"Not really."

"What about that sun up there? Surely *that's* a miracle. Without it continually burning away up there in the sky, everything down here would die. Everything! Can you feel that morning breeze, Bryce. How marvelous! It's a miracle too. So are those fantastic clouds in the sky, the warm rays of the sun, and the very air itself, with every single breath we take. Who can possibly explain it? It's all perfectly inexplicable. That's why we call it a miracle."

I was just a child back then, and he was definitely dumbing things down, but it still had its intended effect. I could feel my next breath rising within me. I could feel the life-giving warmth of the sun on my face and hands.

"Think about this, Bryce," he suggested. "Imagine if the world we lived in was nothing but a flat endless colorless desert. Can you picture that in your mind?"

Which I did.

With all the powers of a child's imagination, I conjured such a lifeless place in my mind.

"Well, if we really *did* live in such a world, we'd still think it was the most marvelous and beautiful thing that ever existed. We'd think that it was exciting and lovely and mysterious, and we'd write poems about it, and we'd paint it in pictures, and we'd sing songs of gratitude. But, instead, God gave us *this* world, full of so many natural wonders that, eventually, we stop noticing. In a way, it's as if God has given us too much. He puts us in a world so replete with beauty, with miracles, that we become blinded to the miraculous all around us. We lose our appreciation. We lose our gratitude."

"So God made a mistake?" I asked, maybe a bit too precociously.

But he liked my question, and he laughed out loud.

"Yes, it might seem that way, Bryce, but *we're* the ones who make the mistakes. In a way, we intentionally blind ourselves, failing to appreciate what we have. Remember, God expects us to do what's right. To prove ourselves. To prove our love. Even though we fail over and over and over again. First in the Garden of Eden and now in this difficult but still miraculous world. Fortunately, God is merciful. Which is yet another miracle."

I seemed to understand, but he wanted me to "think about it" some more, which I did, on countless occasions, for the rest of my life.

Then, most carefully, the old man took out a small package and opened it in front of me.

"Fudge!"

My most favorite thing in the world.

(Still is.)

Without another word, we each took a piece, letting the chocolate explode its sugars, then ever-so-slowly dissolve in our mouths.

We sat together in our little boat, gently undulating on the waters of the bay, in perfect communion.

"Fudge is a miracle," I said, breaking the silence.

"Absolutely," he agreed, having enjoyed the candy as much as me.

"*Everything* is," he repeated.

I thought of Angelina again.

As soon as we landed in Lisbon, I cruised through customs, found a phone, and called her.

Right on time!

When she picked up, I could hear her hair dryer.

"How's my love?" I asked, before she had a chance to say a word.

She shut off her dryer.

"Missing someone," she said, a bit sleepily, saying, as always, something quite perfect.

I've noticed, by the way, that I tend to overuse that word (perfect) quite a bit ever since I first saw her at Giolitti's eating a strawberry ice cream cone.

So I told her about the Vatican, about the pope, which still seemed hard to believe, and about my uncle's terminal condition. About Portugal. She took it right in stride. Yes, it would probably wreck our weekend together, but she understood how important it was. It was family, after all.

She understood perfectly.

But I still hadn't given up on Cannes. I explained that I'd try to get back to Rome later tonight, or, at the latest, tomorrow evening, so we could still fly to the French coast by midnight. Then we'd still have Saturday and Sunday together. Or Sunday and Monday, if she could skip work on Monday. She thought it was a wonderful idea, either which way, and neither of us gave the slightest thought to the expense of rescheduling our airfares at the last minute. Why should we? We were young, in love, and nothing else mattered. Hopefully, I'd be with her soon, we'd fly off together, just as planned, to sit on the beaches at Cannes and watch the lunar eclipse.

Together.

Which sounded perfect.

"Besides," she said, "you owe me quite a few kisses."

I tried, with admirable effort, not to think about the fact that she was probably standing there naked in her apartment, drying off the wet of her shower, and I also tried not to think about the fact that she'd told me, just a few hours ago, that she wanted "to make love."

It wasn't easy.

"I wish I could give you a few right now," I wished out loud.

"That would be lovely, love."

We said goodbye.

I took an immediate and rather blurry taxi ride to the railroad station, and as soon as I sat down in the train, I fell asleep. I regretted my exhaustion, but I had no choice. I'd never visited Portugal before, and I would have liked to see something of the country, of its countryside, of its people, but I didn't. Eventually, I was awoken by the conductor in Leiria, and, almost immediately, I was back in another taxi, heading into the rolling countryside toward Fatima, an isolated little village named for the daughter of Mohammed. Back in 1917, it was the place where three young shepherds had first seen an angel, then later, on several occasions, the Virgin Mother of Jesus Christ.

Supposedly.

Claims of such heavenly apparitions are, of course, not uncommon. Usually, they're the result of overactive imaginations, excessive religious piety, outright derangement, or pranks or hoaxes. Even as a child, I was wary of the notion of miracles, especially apparitional miracles, but there was no doubt that "something" peculiar had happened at Fatima. Like Lourdes, where there'd been countless and verified miraculous healings to support the claims of young Bernadette Soubirous, Fatima also had much more than the testimony of the three young children to support its claim for authenticity. It was, in fact, the only known publicly-witnessed and pre-announced miracle since the alleged Resurrection of Jesus Christ. Even that most-significant earlier miracle, although clearly prophesied by Jesus Christ, was not fully comprehended by his apostles and disciples until *after* the fact.

Not so at Fatima.

Under intense pressure from the local government, which was rabidly anti-clerical, the little children were told to ask the Lady if she would perform a miracle to verify her appearance, since only the children could actually see the Virgin, which, of course, seemed more than a little bit suspicious. The children did as they were told, and, amazingly, the "Lady in White" agreed.

On October 13, 1917, about a hundred thousand people crowded into the Cova da Iria to witness the miracle. Most of the people were devout rural peasants, but there were also countless skeptics, non-believers, and atheists in attendance, all eager to debunk the apparitions. Even the secular dailies from Lisbon sent their reporters to the little country knoll to finally put an end to the religious nonsense that had incited so much attention across the country.

But things didn't work out as they expected.

In the midst of a rather disconcerting downpour, the oldest child, Lúcia, announced that the Lady was present. She then pointed up at the sky and cried, "Look at the sun!" Immediately, the sun turned a flat-silver color, radiating no apparent heat, so that it was now possible to observe it without pain. Then the impossible happened. The sun began to rapidly rotate in the sky. It seemed to "dance" for a bit, then, suddenly, ominously, it began to plunge downwards toward the Cova, as if hurtling toward a collision with the earth. Everyone saw it. Everyone was terrified. Many cried out in fear. The religious, thinking that the Second Coming was upon them, fell to their knees, and huddled to the ground in prayer. The terrified secularists held their breath, in disbelief, believing that the end of the world had come. Mass death and annihilation hovered directly above all of them. The sun, like a massive wheel of fire, was falling rapidly from the sky. Then, just as suddenly as it had begun, everything was over. The sun reversed itself, quickly resumed its natural position in the sky, and everyone in the Cova, still in shock, realized that they were now perfectly dry. The sun had dried their rain-drenched clothes in a matter of minutes.

The terrifying miracle was over.

The Miracle of the Sun.

What had happened, had definitely "happened," and no one tried to deny that something extraordinary had taken place. Not even the secularists. Not even the newspapers. Some of the reporters, and other skeptics as well, actually converted on the spot. Subsequent facile theories about mass delusion were immediately refuted by the simple fact that the phenomenon had been witnessed in nearby towns by people who had no idea what was going on at the Cova.

On the other hand, of course, the sun hadn't simultaneously plunged towards the streets of New York City, or Bangkok, or Rio, or anywhere else. So *what* did happen in Fatima that day? Well, *something* certainly "happened," and the old man that I was about to visit had no doubt that God had, once again, extended his presence into this little world that we temporarily inhabit. During his years in Coimbra, the old priest had become close friends with Lúcia dos Santos, the oldest of the shepherd children, now a Discalced Carmelite, and, as a result, he'd been invited to serve as the spiritual advisor for the cloistered sisters. More recently, living in the heart of Fatima, he'd become involved in many of the activities at the shrine, serving as the on-site chaplain for the Blue Army, an international organization dedicated to the apparitions, and to the amazing prophecies of the "Lady in White" and their apparent ramifications in the modern world.

Suddenly, my wildly-winding roadtrip through the Portuguese countryside was over, and my taxi pulled up to the front of a handsome monastery on the outskirts of Fatima, not far from Cova da Iria.

At first sight, the place looked a bit extravagant for my rather ascetic uncle, and, when no one answered my persistent rings at the heavy front doors, I followed a narrow stone path around the side of the building and entered into a small cemetery. There was a young woman kneeling amid the stones, apparently weeding the plots, and I headed in her direction.

I was wrong.

She was praying.

There was a small, quite weathered, stone statue of St. Dominic in the midst of the cemetery, and she was kneeling before it in sup-plication, in meditation. I had a mixed reaction. I both respected and pitied the young woman's piety. On the other hand, what the hell was she really praying to? Some monk who'd died back in the Thirteenth Century?

As I came closer, walking past a small mausoleum, I finally saw her face. Her eyes were closed. She was remarkably beautiful. So much so that it stopped me in my tracks. Her dark-black hair was closely cropped, quite unfashionably, but it highlighted her angelic face, her dark complexion, her soft features, and her seeming unworldliness. She was probably around eighteen years old, trim, yet also voluptuous in her shabby loose clothes. There was, on her face, a look of interminable sorrow. I'd often heard of a persistent European cliché that *all* the

Portuguese people have a sad, rather mournful look about them, even though they're also reputed to be among the friendliest people in Europe. Apparently, the Lusitanians have a word for their own perpetual sadness, "*saudade,*" and even though I'd slept through most of my time in Portugal, I'd seen it everywhere.

But this young woman's sadness seemed to transcend anything else that I'd seen so far.

Any kind of national idiosyncrasy.

What was the matter with her?

She opened her eyes.

They were deep, dark, lively, and lovely. She blessed herself and nodded slightly in my direction. Then she smiled, and it knocked me back a bit. It seemed to me that there was *nothing* the matter with this young girl, except for the fact that she was a stunningly beautiful young woman who was wasting her life away in the middle of nowhere, dressed like a peasant, and praying to nothing and no one.

I noticed a rosary in her hand and the brown scapular cords over her shoulders and under her blouse. Again, I felt nothing but an unsettling mix of compassion and pity.

What a waste.

Unfortunately, I only knew two words in Portuguese, and one of them was "*saudade.*"

"Father Sinclair?" I tried.

Immediately, the young girl understood and pointed to a little white and green cottage further down the pathway behind the monastery.

I nodded.

"*Obrigado,*" I said, which was the only other word I knew, meaning "thank you."

She nodded politely.

"They're waiting for you," she said with a lovely Portuguesed English.

She smiled again, and it crushed my heart.

Maybe it's true that this ridiculous world of ours is full of lovely young girls wasting their lives away, but I certainly didn't want to think about it.

So I didn't.

I turned away and started walking towards the little house nestled in a distant grove of overhanging trees. Out front, there was a long black car, a limousine of some kind, sitting in the shade. Through the tinted glass, I could see the driver, waiting patiently, reading a newspaper.

This was definitely the house of death.

. . . and oddly enough, I was fully aware of it at the time of my ordination. In fact, I'd been aware of my "problem," and its only possible solution, my entire life.

Even as a young child, I recognized the fact that I was, in some way, unbalanced, and that I needed to rectify the situation. That I needed, in some way, to cure myself. Since the problem, my condition, my imbalance, was spiritual, not psychological, I naturally found myself inexorably drawn to the church for rectification and resolution.

Even as a young boy, I was fully aware that there were two things that clearly set me off from my parents: an inordinate self-absorption and a harrowing discontent. Naturally, it was the latter problem that most disturbed me as a child. Why were my parents so generally content? And the rest of our family as well? How had they managed to fashion themselves into such basically kind, thoughtful, and easygoing people? How had they managed to achieve a serene sense of equilibrium in their lives? How had they managed not just to acquiesce to the faith, but to live it fully, in a most natural and casual day-in-and-day-out Christian Catholicism?

I didn't know the answer, but I was determined to find out. I wanted to be just like my parents. I wanted to be content. Neither of them, of course, had any idea that every, single, pervasive discontent of my youth was naturally exacerbated by the stark and obvious contrast between my own dark disquiets and their seemingly-effortless contentment. Their ubiquitous presence in my life was a constant and continual reminder of my own inner failing, my spiritual disruptions, but I bore them no grudge whatsoever. I actually admired them both and wished to emulate the way in which they led their lives. In all honesty, I harbored no resentment. In fact, I suffered no reflexive rages against anything at all. Not against the world itself, not against the Roman Catholic Church, not even against myself. Quite simply, there was never any kind of excuse-making. My situation, in fact, seemed quite obvious. There was discontent in my heart, and it was clearly my own problem, and it was entirely up to me to overcome it. Subsume it. Since the fundamental source of all discontents (and the source, in fact, of all human disability) is spiritual, and since I loved and admired the church, I sought her out, vigorously, for both sustenance and guidance.

Yet all of this, of course, logically exacerbated the other problem: the excessive self-absorption. Or maybe, in some way, they were two sides of the same coin. If you're discontent, then you're naturally hyper-aware that you're discontent, and such a hyper-awareness naturally reinforces the intensity of your own preoccupations with yourself. Which I knew wasn't good. Which I knew wasn't healthy. Which I clearly sensed, even in the midst of the self-absorption itself. Which, of course, made things even worse. Besides, hadn't Jesus Christ clearly commanded us to concern ourselves with the well-being of others? So I strove to follow his precepts as assiduously as I was able.

What does a child do under such circumstances?

I was perceptive enough to realize that my spiritual doubts and confusions (like fixating on passages in the Bible which seemed to contradict each other, or allowing myself to dwell on the perceived and tangible absence of God in the natural world around me, and so on) were probably just the result of my rather obvious precocity. My parents, in fact, were only moderately intelligent people, and my own seemingly unlimited intellectual capacity seemed, at least to me, the most reasonable and logical source of my problem. Obviously, I was "thinking" too much. I was over-intellectualizing everything, over-obsessing, and turning myself into a silly little pedant.

So I tried to deal with it.

But I knew that I couldn't be something less than what I was. Or something different. In other words, I knew that I couldn't actually shut down my hyperactive mind, so, instead, I'd have to find a way to redirect it. I'd have to fully absorb myself into holy mother church, especially her rigors, her asceticisms, and her demanding rationalities.

Obviously, there couldn't *be any contradictions in the Bible, or in the endless labyrinths of Catholic doctrine. Certainly Aquinas, the greatest intellectual genius in the history of the world, would have never subsumed himself into a kind of clever irrationality. So I decided to follow in his path. I would learn. I would learn* everything. *And I would learn to be patient. I would seek out all the reasons, all the explanations, all the subtitles of discourse, and all the rest of it.*

Which I did.

It was exhilarating. It was absolutely mind-boggling to discover that the faith I'd inherited from my parents, as if by accident, was actually the most spectacular and challenging and fascinating intellectual conundrum in the world, in the entire history of the world. Blindly, I'd rather fortuitously stumbled into the midst of some kind of stupendous billion-square chess game, while everyone else was moronically playing tiddlywinks.

In conjunction with all of these marvelous intellectual rigors, I also undertook a rather systematic pietistic rigor. Throughout my entire childhood, initiating at the age of five, I'd been gradually developing an ever-increasing, ever-demanding ascetic discipline for myself. I was convinced, following St. Francis (the Salesian), that "It's a thousand times better to die with the Lord, than to live without Him." So my daily rule consisted of increasing mortifications, multifarious sacrifices, forced submissions to the needs of my parents, intense prayer, and devotional readings. For some reason, devotional tracts never had much of an appeal to either my mind or my innate nature. Quite naturally, I preferred theological disputation, speculation, and extrapolation. As a consequence,

I forced myself to read exactly what I preferred not to read. For the betterment of my soul.

Almost all of this activity, and certainly the rigor of it, I concealed from my parents. I knew that it was prideful, sinful, to make an ostentation of one's spiritual exercises, and I was also, in my heart, not quite certain how they'd react. They were devout but rather spontaneous Catholics, living a faith that came to them very naturally. Being Roman Catholic, being a faithful Catholic, seemed as natural and instinctive to their lives as being a man or being a woman or taking one's next breath.

I, on the other hand, had to work quite a bit harder.

I didn't mind.

Not at all.

On the contrary, I exalted in the adventure of it, even though I was always conscious that my other problem, the self-preoccupation, remained essentially unabated. At first, I worried about it quite a bit, but eventually, I concluded, maybe a bit too conveniently, that God had given me the mind he'd given me, and that I should just use it and not worry about it so much.

Naturally, the priesthood was a foregone conclusion.

The only question was which order? Should I follow in the footsteps of St Francis? Or Ignatius? Or Dominic, as had Thomas Aquinas? The Jesuits, of course, naturally appealed to me as a kind of elitist brotherhood of intellectual warriors, but I also wondered if I should avoid the Society for the very reasons that made it so appealing. For several years, I agonized over the problem, then finally made my choice, and my parents were delighted. It was a great personal pleasure to see them finally indulge in a little bit of that natural human pride which they so seldom permitted themselves in their quiet, humble, daily lives.

That's why I became a priest. To minister to myself. To deal with my own sense of spiritual deficiency; my disinclination to natural piety; my complete incomprehensibility in the face of the most primary of all Christian concepts: submissiveness; and, finally, my own innate (almost compulsive) tendency to skepticism.

Even rebellion.

It worked.

At least, for a while. Eventually, of course, I had to face the unfortunate fact that despite the stupendous majesty of the faith, and all its intellectual sublimity, and all its unparalleled historical significance, it was really, at base, as I'd seemed to intuit at the age of five, nothing more than a fantastical fairy tale.

So what had happened on that crucial day?

I'm certain that you're all wondering about it.

Wondering why it happened on that particular specific day, on the Thursday after Pentecost, in the sixth year of my priesthood. Well, I'm afraid the answer is rather disappointing, because nothing much happened at all. Certainly nothing dramatic.

I'd been over at the cancer ward that morning, easing some barely-conscious terminal into the afterlife. I read his Last Rites, consoled his family, and everything went as well as those things can possibly go. There was nothing particularly unusual or upsetting about it. The old guy was a billion years old, his body and his mind were completely shot, and he'd apparently lived a rather decent life, earning the love and respect of his family. He'd also believed emphatically in Jesus Christ and the paradise that his Redeemer had promised him.

Finally, after he'd fallen off into the blackness, I left the hospital and headed back to the rectory, walking down to the beach, as I often did. It was a lovely day. The Mediterranean was a miraculous deep-blue, and there were enough majestic clouds drifting across the sky to softly mute the harsh edges of the sunlight. Without thinking, I stopped and stared at the sea, just a lonely solitary figure, a little priest in a black cassock and a white collar.

As often happened in my daily life, a short text suddenly popped into my mind. Nothing peculiar, nothing dramatic, nothing particularly relevant.

It was Romans 8:11.

> *And if the Spirit of him, who raised up Jesus from the dead, dwell in you: he that raised up Jesus Christ from the dead, shall quicken also your mortal bodies, because of his spirit dwelling in you.*

Now, of course, I have no intention of insulting your intelligence by going into the whole endlessly-discussed rigmarole about "Well, if Christ really is God, then why did he need some other 'he' (the Father? the Spirit? whatever?) to raise him up?" Why didn't he just do it himself? Why did he need the other "he"?

I realize that this is a pretty worn-out sleight-of-hand. Among thousands, right? And I'm sure that we all know the various stock refutations. For example, that Christ did such things vis-à-vis the Father. As with

"Father, if thou wilt, remove this chalice," or "Eli, Eli, lamma sabacthani?" etc. That such things were done as exemplification, to provide a model for us to follow in submission to the incomprehensible mystery of the personhood(s) of God, of which Christ was and is, in the theological mystery, both separate and equal and of one and the same essence, substance, being, and unity.

I have no doubt that I could demolish such a misreading of the resurrectional reference in Romans as well as anyone in the room, as well as anyone in the world, for that matter, but it still occurs to me, as it did on the beach that day, "So what?" So what if I can refute it, step by step, with some clever theological song-and-dance?

Let's face it, if you don't behave like God, then you're not God. It's just that simple. If you can't raise yourself up, then somebody else has to do it for you. And if that happens, then the whole, fantastic, amazing, endless house-of-cards tumbles to the ground, all over me, all over the beach, all over you, all over everything. Two thousand years of breathtaking explication is suddenly undone. Not to mention the whole of my own little life of self-willed supplication, of submission, of intellectual subservience.

Suddenly, somehow, someone somewhere had tipped over the chess board.

The someone was me.

As previously mentioned, I'm fully aware that this little recollection of my "turning," of my initial refutation, is rather disappointing. Not very memorable at all. That one should initiate a life of contumacious (to use Augustine's term) apostasy, with all it subsequent heresy, on the basis of a stroll down the beach, on the basis of a little phrase from the Tarsusian, really does seem rather ridiculous and rather mundane. But the relief was not. Neither, I can assure you, was the conviction. My sudden and irrevocable alteration of belief was predicated on a sincerely honest and categorical conviction. Regardless of how it came to pass, I'd suddenly found the strength to undo myself, to cast off all the garbage and the self-delusion and the pretense, and to irrevocably recreate myself and my entire existence. The dullish specifics of how it actually came about are both immaterial and irrelevant. I didn't reorder my entire life on the basis of some dumb little text in the Douay Romans; I reordered my life because I was able, at that particular moment in time, on that particular sunny afternoon, to finally see the world, with all its extraordinary loveliness and depravity, for exactly what it was.

And remains:

Godless.

Chapter 4

Deathbed

(Friday, August 4th)

No, I don't repent. Absolutely not! Who the hell would I be repenting to?

The door of the little house was slightly open.

Everything was perfectly silent. Inside and out. Maybe for that reason, I decided not to knock. Quietly, I pushed the front door open and stepped inside the tiny one-room cottage.

The small white room was meticulously neat and spartan. The bed, which seemed quite high, probably a hospital bed, was set off to my right, slightly off-center in the room against the far wall. Above the bed, there was a small picture of Jesus Christ. Actually, it was a detail from a famous picture by Heinrich Hofmann portraying some kind of encounter in the New Testament, maybe the betrayal in the Garden of Gethsemane. Even though I couldn't remember the entire picture, I certainly recognized the detail, the face of Christ, because my parents had a similar picture hanging in the small parlor of our home in Ocean City. Maybe my uncle had given them the picture many years ago?

Maybe as a present? Or maybe it was the other way around? Maybe my parents had once given my uncle the picture that was now hanging on the blank wall over his deathbed?

Whatever the case, I knew the Hofmann portrait well, always feeling rather ambivalent about it. Yes, the German artist had certainly conceived Christ's sorrowful face in an unforgettably striking way, deeply complex, emotionally powerful. But maybe it was *too* complex. When I was a boy, I would often stare at the picture and believe that Christ was staring back at me, full of a weary compassion, flush with mercy, with a "They know not what they do" kind of look. But other times, I'd stare at the exact same picture, and I'd see the "other side" of Christ, the God who was fully horrified by sin, by rejection, by betrayal, by all human frailty, and not just that of Judas Iscariot, or whomever Christ was looking at in the larger picture. On those days, Christ was clearly "Christ the Judge," inexorably compelled to deal with sin exactly as it needed to be dealt with.

It was a bit unnerving.

The other walls in the room were totally blank. White and blank. Surprisingly, there was no crucifix anywhere. On the little table near the head of the bed, there was a glass, half-full of water, and a few envelopes. Oddly, there were only a few books in the room, maybe a dozen or so, sitting stacked on the floor in a far corner, and there seemed to be no kitchen. Maybe the old man did his studies at the monastery. Maybe he ate his meals there as well.

My uncle, my great-uncle, my namesake, Fr. Bryce Sinclair was lying flat-out on his back in the high bed, beneath a single white sheet, with only his head protruding. Even under the cover of the white sheet, the shrunken, emaciate remains of this once vigorous and extraordinary man were shocking to see. I was horrified by what my uncle had become. I looked closer at the old man's head. His face, completely immobile, with eyes shut, seemed a cadaverous death mask. It was definitely the same man who'd taken me on our little adventures when I was a boy in Maryland, but it was also the revoltingly grotesque reduction of what that man had once been. Illness had completely ravaged him, mercilessly, and death had enveloped his meager remains.

Sitting at the right side of the bed, against the right wall, were two perfectly stationary figures. Oddly enough, neither of them even bothered to look when I entered the room. Surely they knew I was there. Surely they couldn't have cared less. Their grief was pulverizing.

One, the closest one, was a priest in his late forties, trim not tall, rather fastidious, with jet-black hair and eyes that seemed to peer out fixedly into the nothingness before him. Despite the depths of his preoccupation, he projected an air of interior anxiety. He had the lean-and-hungry look of the intellectual. His absorption in the gruesome scene before him was total.

The same could be said of the second figure, Vincente Cardinal Barcelos. In the whole wide world, I could probably recognize and identify only one or two Catholic cardinals, and Cardinal Barcelos of Lisbon was one of them. The man's face was everywhere, especially whenever the pope fell sick, since he was considered an obvious candidate for succession. He was popular, moderate, diplomatic, contemporary, and just the right age, a youthful sixty-five or so. He'd somehow managed to make himself pleasing to all the varying curia camps, and most everyone, both inside and outside the Vatican, expected him to be the next pope.

Naturally, I was quite astonished to see the cardinal sitting in the little room at the head of my uncle's bed. But, then again, why not? It seemed perfectly reasonable that they'd probably met during my uncle's decades-long exile in Portugal, and that the cardinal had, most likely, come to pay his respects. Maybe even to hear the dying priest's final confession.

Like the younger priest to his left, Barcelos sat on a simple, metal folding-chair, completely lost and contemplative, seemingly imprisoned within an impenetrable shell of staggering grief. He was completely static and immobile, as if catatonic, as if struck by lightning. It seemed to me that maybe something significant had already happened in the room, not long before I'd entered, and that it had affected, profoundly, if not fundamentally altered, the two men present. Maybe it was the obvious fact of my uncle's death, but surely men such as these had witnessed death after countless death in the course of their long ministries.

Having no idea what to do, I nodded politely at the two priests, who either didn't see me or simply decided not to pay any attention. Then, unobtrusively, carefully, I took a seat in the third folding chair, the farthest from the head of the bed, next to the younger priest. I had the feeling that the chair had been placed there just for me. It seemed not only that the vacant chair was waiting specifically for me, but it also seemed, for some inexplicable reason, as though everyone else in the room, despite their self-absorption, was, similarly, waiting specifically for me.

Just as the young girl in the cemetery had said.

"They're waiting for you."

Still exhausted from my trip, still stunned by the appearance of my uncle, I settled back into the silence, becoming like the others in the room, absolutely motionless, as if paralyzed in the face of the blackness of death.

Then I noticed something odd, off to my left, across the room, in front of an open back door. A little peasant boy was sitting on the ground eating an ice cream cone, quietly looking through a group of holy cards, some of which he held in his free hand, some of which he'd placed on the floor in front of him. He was probably around eight years old, and I naturally assumed he was Portuguese, given his complexion, dark hair, and dark eyes. He was a cute little kid, a bit pudgy, with a sweet face. He seemed completely oblivious to the scene at the deathbed across the room, and the two priests, in a similar manner, seemed completely unaware or impervious to the little boy's presence.

Somehow, I seemed to understand that the little boy was just an innocent child eating ice cream and playing contentedly by himself on the floor of the room. The fact that death was also present in the room made no difference whatsoever. Maybe he was the son of the caretaker? Or the gardener? Or someone like that? Maybe he'd grown close to my charismatic uncle over the past few years? But whatever the reason for his presence in the room, I was grateful. In truth, I would have preferred to walk across the room, sit down, and play with the little boy. Maybe even go outside? Maybe kick around a soccer ball for a while? Because *anything*, absolutely anything, was better than what I was doing right now, sitting at the baleful banks of Acheron.

Eventually, I forced the distractions from my mind. It was time to face the fact that I'd arrived too late. That I'd missed the opportunity to say all the things that I'd been planning to say to my dying uncle. To let him know how much I loved him. To apologize for falling out of touch. To ask him to forgive whatever he felt might need forgiving. Throughout the entire exhausting trip from the Vatican, whenever I was awake, I was constantly deliberating about the various things I wanted to say to the old man. I wanted to walk right into his bedroom, hold his hand, stand beside him, and try to give him, as best I could, some kind of comfort.

Some kind of love.

I was also determined, as requested, to record his "final message." Whatever it might be.

But things hadn't worked out that way.

I'd arrived too late, and even the pope hadn't been able to make things right. It now seemed as though my entire trip was a waste of time. I'd raced from Rome to Fatima for nothing. Yet, deep in my heart, despite the terrible disappointment, despite the frustration, I also felt gratified that I'd made the attempt. I'd done my best to get here as quickly as I could, and even now, under these less-than-satisfying circumstances, it felt pleasurable, once again, to be in the presence of this good and holy man. If there *really* was some kind of benevolent God out there, surely this marvelous and decent man would now be rewarded for his selfless life.

The sheet moved.

Reflexively, I jerked back in my chair.

The lifeless body stirred in its bed.

I was shocked.

Then I was shocked by my own stupidity. The old man was *still* alive. Just barely. Lingering somewhere at the portals of death. The other men in the room grew intensely alert. Obviously, they'd known that the old man was still alive, and they'd been waiting in some kind of mutually suspended animation, waiting for something to happen.

Almost instinctively, apparently unnoticed, I pressed the "play" button on the little recorder in my jacket pocket.

Waiting for I knew not what.

He spoke.

But it wasn't the voice of the man that I'd known in my youth. It was the deathly cackle of a voice rising from the grave. It was harsh, superior, devoid of any semblance of beneficence:

I concluded, the Thursday after Pentecost, that there was no God . . .

I was stunned.

Horrified.

My heart crashed around in my chest. My breath was labored, and I found it impossible to comprehend what I was hearing.

What *was* I hearing?

The seemingly unrepentant confession of a man, a priest, an exemplar of Christian virtue, who'd obviously led a surreptitious and double life, who'd led a second life of comprehensive and self-willed deception and deceit, and, amazingly, he now seemed quite proud of it.

I've only been sick-to-my-stomach a few times in my life, but I suddenly felt ill and violently feverish. My head hurt at the temples, and I thought I might actually vomit and fall to the floor, but I didn't. I sat right where I was, immobile, and managed to maintain some kind of barely-adequate control, listening carefully to every single word of my uncle's apostasy, his heresy, his loveless sexuality.

It was revolting, disgusting.

Yes, I'd fallen away from the Church, but I'd never pretended otherwise. Not even for the benefit of my parents. But this conscienceless man had duped everyone. Everyone, everywhere. People all over the world. After all, he'd become one of the most beloved and respected Christians in all of Christendom. How could he have done such a thing? How had he been able to live with himself? How could he lie there in the clutches of death and expose himself with such remorseless and demonic self-satisfaction?

It was terrible.

Everything about it was terrible, but what felt the most hurtful and repulsive to me personally was the fact that the old man had specifically called me here to be at his bedside. He'd obviously wanted his nephew, who'd always admired him, if not idolized him, to hear and record every single repulsive word. He'd even used the pope to achieve his ends, and he'd waited ever-so-patiently at the portals of death, at the portals of hell, until I finally arrived. Somehow, he'd managed to fend off the terminality of his death in order to expose himself to his nephew.

His namesake.

It was cunning, callous, and inexplicable.

Thank God, I thought to himself, that my father and my mother and my sister and all the rest of our family weren't here this afternoon to witness these revolting disclosures. At least, I could be grateful for that. Now they'll *never* know about it. I'll make sure of it. I'll lie without compunction. I'll tell them that my Uncle-Father died exactly as they would have expected him to die. Like a saint. Like a Christian paragon. So, maybe, oddly enough, everything was for the best. If anyone had to hear this garbage, it was probably best that it was me.

Probably.

As I continued to listen to my uncle's alien almost otherworldly voice attempt to explicate his endless catalogue of perversities, it occurred to me that the man was probably insane. Maybe his cancers had made him this way. Maybe his loss of his faith had damaged his mind. Or maybe he'd always been psychotic, and no one had recognized it. Maybe, in some crucially significant way, the old man wasn't fully culpable for what he'd done in the past, for what he was saying now, for whatever he was trying to do to everyone present in the room, all of whom I assume had been specifically summoned.

Yet deep within my heart, I knew that psychotic derangement was the easy way out, the excuse that everyone falls back on when confronted with unmitigated evil. "Oh, it's not *really* his fault, he's mentally unbalanced." "Oh, he's not *really* morally culpable for what he's done." "Or what he's doing." Well, maybe it was true in a number of rare cases (I certainly believed in the reality of mental derangement), but sitting here, right now, at this particular moment in time, I had every reason to believe that the half-dead skeletal man, lying beneath his white sheet, on top of his high hospital bed, had full and complete control of all his faculties. That he'd done everything that he'd ever done in his previous life with a cool, calm, intellectual calculation, as a consequence of his fully-realized force of will, of his powerfully-asserted freedom of will.

The voice stopped.

Finally.

A hollow oppressive silence filled the room. I glanced at the priest sitting next to me, who sat perfectly still and expressionless, as if his mind was racing a billion miles a second trying to fathom everything that he'd just heard. Then I looked at the cardinal. He seemed mortally wounded, temporarily shut-down, as if he'd been somehow cast into the rank amphitheater of hell.

Unexpectedly, from across the room, the little boy spoke. He spoke with the remarkable innocence of a child, having finished his ice cream, still glancing down at his holy pictures. He also spoke with a kind of vocal impediment that was difficult for me to isolate since I didn't know the language.

"Por que você se tornou padre?" the boy asked.

Even though I had no facility with Portuguese, I recognized the Italian cognates and understood what the boy was asking:

"Why did you become a priest?"

The question seemed extremely peculiar, especially since the little boy showed no real interest in the old man's response. Once again, as before, the cardinal and the other priest paid absolutely no attention to the little boy, not even glancing in his direction.

But the near-dead-thing lying on his deathbed responded immediately, as naturally as if the cardinal had asked the question.

Once again, I was forced to listen to yet another supercilious discourse from the cadaver's death's-head.

I became a priest for the same reason that a psychiatrist becomes a psychiatrist . . .

Yes, I was no longer a true believer in the faith, or any faith for that matter, but I can still recognize *sin* in this world. I'm fully aware that sin, though never excusable, is both ubiquitous and absolutely fundamental to our natural concupiscence, our innate desires and impulses. But human sins are *not* created equal, as Dante and the illuminist monks had so meticulously illustrated in the middle ages. Maybe if my father was sitting here, he would have been most repulsed by the apostasy. Maybe if my mother was here, she would have been most scandalized by the sexual crudities. Maybe if my sister Ronnie was here, she would have been most horrified by the man's stupendous irredeemable vanity. But for me, the most shocking shock of all the afternoon's seemingly endless compendium of shocks was the heresy.

It's one thing to abandon one's faith. It's quite another matter to spend the rest of one's life willfully trying to subvert it and pervert it. Ironically, I was fully cognizant of the facts of doctrinal heresy *because* of my uncle, the one lying there before me, who'd made such doctrinal distinctions perfectly clear when I was a young boy. Whenever we were alone together, especially when we talked about religion, I always directed the discussion toward the subject that I found most fascinating:

the heretics. They were brazen, they were creative, they were fantastic public sinners, and my uncle never once disapproved of my interest.

My curiosity.

"To be a Catholic, you need to apprehend the enemy," he said one time. "And who's the enemy, Bryce?"

"Satan."

"Yes, Satan and all his earthly generals. The Heresiarchs."

For my eleventh birthday, my uncle sent me a pristine copy of Lawson's old, rather rare (1894), and thumpingly orthodox *The Heresiarchs: The Scourge of the Mystical Body of Christ*. I can still remember just how excited I was receiving such a mysterious book in the mail from faraway Europe, and how I devoured it immediately. Exalting in it. Maybe for the wrong reasons. As soon as I'd finished, I immediately read it all over again, trying, as best I could, to fathom some of the more subtle theological disputations. In an especially creepy way, the presently dying priest had actually been preparing his nephew for his amazing deathbed revelations nearly fifteen years ago, alerting me to the dangers and the ever-tempting intellectual stimulations of the great theological perversities of the legendary heresiarchs.

Finally, the evil priest wrapped-up his recollections about his fateful stroll down the beach and his deadly encounter with the verse from Romans. Once again, another eerie silence filled the room. Once again, no one moved. Once again, the little boy paid absolutely no attention to anything that was taking place across the room.

After what seemed like an interminable stretch of time, the cardinal broke the silence.

Up until that moment, ever since I'd entered the room, the cardinal had stared fixedly, in shock, at the skullish face that protruded from the white sheet on the bed in front of him. But the eyes of the two old priests had never actually met since the one who was seemingly-dead never moved, even when he spoke. He lay there on his back, staring upwards at the white ceiling, as if he couldn't move, as if he might be blind, as if he didn't care.

At last, Barcelos spoke, weakly, with an accented English, as if from the lowest levels of his spiritual depths. He spoke as if he'd been doomed from the genesis to say what he was now compelled to say, as if he was already aware, without doubt, the answer to the question he was obligated to ask.

"Do you repent?"

No, I don't repent. Absolutely not! Who the hell would I be repenting to?

The cardinal made no response. He was a man without resource, without sustenance. He'd been crushed by the pulverizing power of the one lying in front of him, completely incapacitated, whose flesh, it seemed, had already begun to decay.

The voice of the heretic continued:

. . . To you? To the likes of you? Or to the Christ-who-doesn't-even-exist? And why? What's the point? To make you feel "better" about things? To make you feel as though something had finally been accomplished this sunny afternoon? Well, forget it. Penance provides for the needs of the

penitent and for the equally important needs of the priest as well, but I have absolutely no need for either of those sorry needs.

Whenever I'm compelled to contemplate the absurdities of confession, I recall Basilides' rather sweeping, somewhat parallel dismissal of Christian martyrdom as a perfectly pointless gesture since it's misguidedly directed at Christ. Not at the Cyrene. Which, of course, makes it perfectly ludicrous, and since you've read my books, there's no need to clarify the point any further.

As for myself, my actions, and my life, I have absolutely no regrets. None. Which I'm sure might surprise you. I don't even, for example, regret the fact that I came to the truth when I did and not sooner, because all the stages of my progression have had their pleasures and rewards. In time, of course, I finally decided, in effect, to roll the Pascalian dice off the table, and I'm perfectly content with the ramifications of that decision. I've enjoyed everything, even the difficulties, and I've discovered, over time, that I've become quite capable of anything and everything.

Even, it might amuse you to contemplate, murder. Yes, there were more than a few times when that foolishly stubborn Geneviève was sitting in front of me in her early pregnancy and stubbornly refusing my advice, and the thought ran through my mind that putting an end to her life might have been mutually beneficial. Actually, I believe that I could have effected the result quite easily, quite efficiently, but I decided against it. It wasn't really my style, was it? And style is extremely important in this life, especially with people like me. Murdering that silly girl seemed much too messy. Much too easy. It was also, in a curious way, much too intimate. So I decided against it. Not because it was wrong, but because it wasn't comfortably congruous with my own specific nature, my sense of fastidiousness, my admitted need for distance and disengagement.

As for moral questions regarding the sinfulness of the act, how curious it seems that only two months later, Geneviève would, of course, decide to murder herself in Salzburg. Maybe if I'd been so inclined to suffocate her earlier, along with that other minuscule life swelling within her, on top of my rectory bed, our one-time "field of love," she wouldn't have had to suffer through the subsequent abortion, the guilt-racked aftermath, our traumatic break-up, and whatever other hells she finally endured in Salzburg. Maybe, in a way, I was remiss in my duty to that young girl. Maybe her death should have come earlier. And, let's face it, in retrospect, does it really matter whether it was her hands or mine?

Or if it was cancer or a speeding truck or an act of god?

Besides, as I think you're finally starting to apprehend, I much prefer the murder of the soul. The body is surely the useful temple of the sensual, but the soul is the very fundamental essence of the human being. As a consequence, disrupting, altering, or even killing the latter, is far more intellectually challenging and stimulating and satisfying than the former.

"He who puts doubt in the mind of the believer, alters his life forever."

I do hope you don't mind me quoting myself.

It comes from my forthcoming book, my opus, in fact, called Rennes-le-Château: Le mystère du Christ, *which has already been printed and will be released to the public tomorrow morning in Lisbon, Rome, and Paris simultaneously. I expect it to be quite the bestseller. I also expect that more than a few sorry souls will be greatly altered by the book.*

In my own biased and rather immodest opinion, I'm not sure if Christ will ever recuperate. At least, as "God." At least, as the second person of the Blessed Trinity.

The book, of course, clearly illustrates, very effectively, what a nice fellow he was. After all, he was certainly charismatic, wise, forgiving, and potentially everybody's best friend, but, in the end, he still wants the damned cup lifted, right? "Remove this cup." He's still looking for a helping hand. From something above and beyond himself. So once again, it's been a distinct pleasure to mitigate the stature of Christ. To mitigate the "god" in the Christian god.

Have I succeeded? Or is it just a wishful vanity? After all, let's be honest, more than a few renegades have set their sights on Jesus Christ and come back empty-handed. Where are they all now? Completely forgotten. Yet, all around us, everywhere, we can see the ubiquitous churches, steeples, crosses, and crucifixes. The ubiquitous Christ. But, of course, as I mentioned earlier, that's always the great mistake. You can't "undo" Christ. That's impossible. Nothing will ever eradicate the Nazarene. On the other hand, it might be possible to "alter" him a bit. To change him a bit. To distort perceptions. To knock him down a notch or two. To make him more human. More like ourselves at our very best. More likeable, more personable, and far less godlike.

It used to be believed that the great heresiarchs had three things in common. The first was a forceful personality, maybe even a characteristic greatness (after all, it was Augustine who said, "None save great men have been the authors of heresy"); the second was a rapport with the contemporary weltanschauung; and the third was political support (would anybody still know who blundering Martin Luther was today if it wasn't for Frederick of Saxony?). But the Modernists, despite their embarrassing failures, have proven that, in contemporary times, it's possible to effect an effective heresy without either the first or the third prerequisites. Teilhard, admittedly, had a bit of a flair, but he was no Arius. In today's world, only a few academic pinheads even know who Chardin was, but back in the Fourth Century, the mighty name of Arius was on the lips of every single person in the worth-knowing world. As for requirement number three, yes, the Modernists got some useful coverage and patronage from their moles in the curia, as well as the corrupted hierarchy of the Society of Jesus, but they certainly had no Emperor Antonius Pius standing behind them, as did Basilides in the Second Century.

Modern heresy, in my opinion, can successfully metastasize and per-petuate itself throughout the body of the church as long as it's appropriate to the times, which means that it's decadent, undemanding, intellectual-ly frivolous, and, as I've already discussed, highly imaginative. As long as it strikes deeply at what still remains our most craved and primordial necessity, even superseding physical nourishment, our fundamental need for a dramatic and creatively gratifying spirituality.

So, will the world still know my name (my penname) a hundred years from now? Or a thousand? I really don't know. I suspect that Cyre-nianism will always remain broadly appealing, usefully challenging. I suspect that it will last forever, in fact, but maybe that's just my own vanity speaking. By the way, I've got no problem with vanity, either. I'm perfectly content with my own sense of self-importance and hubris, fully aware that it's often excessive and overdone. As Heywood reminds us in his excellent Proverbs, *"Every cock is proud on his own dunghill." Yes, fine, sure, I'm perfectly comfortable with that. Yes, I'm unabashedly proud, unashamedly, and yes, I very much like my own dunghill. I've created it myself, and I've found it quite marvelous.*

When the blackness soon comes, when the stink of death falls over me, I'll regret nothing. I'll also miss nothing, except the pleasures: the intellectual stimulations, the fine foods, the whores. Life, whatever it is, gives us numerous good things, and I've willingly and most enthusiastically sunk myself into its greatest pleasures. If I was inclined to believe in God, I'd be quite prepared to thank him for his beneficence.

Which is, I suppose a good place to end.

To wrap things up.

Why don't we let that stand as my final blasphemy?

Then, after a brief moment of silence, there was a final continuation.

The one will be a saint.

The one will go to hell.

The one will be a pope.

And the one will serve the prophet. Amen.

II.

PENANCE

"Proportionate mortification, internal or external, imposed by one's confessor, undertaken in atonement for the temporal punishment due to one's sins."

Chapter 5

Crucifix

(Friday, August 4th)

The old man finished.

He shut his eyes.

Once again, he was perfectly motionless. A weird preternatural silence filled the room.

Like both of the priests, I was completely devastated, crushed by the sheer weight and expansiveness of the old man's final confession. I was also completely baffled by his final litany. What *were* those four, short, declarative sentences? What were they supposed to mean? Were they a prophecy of some kind? If so, what did they refer to? And how might they specifically relate to the old man's confession?

Besides, on what grounds could an apostate presume to prophesy?

Maybe *that* was his final blasphemy, which was made even more bizarre by the undeniable fact that my uncle's voice had dramatically altered at the very end, when he'd recited his peculiar litany. Suddenly, his voice became much softer, much calmer, more resigned, without a trace of its previous sarcasm, its previous self-aggrandizement. In those final few moments, he sounded exactly like the man and the priest that I'd once known, but, of course, both the mode and the meaning of his concluding remarks were completely ambiguous, maybe even irrational. Maybe just the ranting gibberish of a tortured soul writhing within its death throes.

I had no idea, but the stark reality of my present situation, and everything that the old man had said, made his final brief comments seem both inconsequential and superfluous.

Nothing more than a curiosity.

I sat in the aftermath, stunned and helpless, not even certain if the old man was living or dead, wishing that I could find some possible way to disbelieve everything that I'd just heard, or, at least, push it out of my battered mind. In a futile effort to distract myself, I glanced across the room looking for the little boy, but he was gone. The only possible glimmer of comfort that I'd been able to find within this terrible place had now left me alone, probably exiting through the back door. Even the child's holy cards were gone. Then, for a brief moment, I wondered if the little boy had actually been there at all. Momentarily, I doubted myself, even though I knew it was preposterous. I'm not the kind of person who's prone to unrealities. Hallucinations. As a matter of fact, I can't remember a single waking delusion in my entire life. But today, obviously, was unlike any other day.

Finally, the cardinal rose from his small folding chair. He seemed, at last, to have overcome his paralytic inertia. He also seemed to have made some kind of resolution. Immediately, he glanced over at the younger priest. Then at me. We both understood, and we rose from our seats in unison, then retreated to the front door, leaving the cardinal alone with the dead.

Nothing was said.

Numbly, mechanically, I followed the silent priest out the main door onto the front porch of the tiny isolated cottage. Instantly, the bright Lusitanian sun flashed painfully into my eyes, and I was suddenly overcome with exhaustion. Whatever had happened in that room had not only crushed my spirit, it had left me physically debilitated. Fortunately, there was a small wooden chair on the porch, and since the distracted priest didn't seem interested, I slumped down wearily.

For several moments, the preoccupied priest stood motionless at the edge of the porch, looking off towards the distant countryside. He said nothing. He seemed completely absorbed in his own tortured yet carefully controlled thoughts. I assumed that the pensive priest had been some kind of protégé of my uncle, although he definitely wasn't Portuguese. Maybe they'd met in Rome. Maybe, more recently, they'd met in Fatima, which is always flush with visiting priests from all over the world.

I naturally wondered if the silent priest had ever suspected any of the atrocities that we'd just heard from my uncle's deathbed. I also wondered if the man's faith had been shaken. I wouldn't be surprised. I felt a powerful compassion for the suffering priest standing in front of me. Then, rather abruptly, the man stepped down from the porch, without saying a word, and walked away, heading for the monastery. He'd said nothing the entire time, and, as a matter of fact, he'd never even acknowledged my presence. Which, under any other circumstances, would have seemed exceedingly rude, but I was completely understanding. After everything that had happened, I could certainly forgive the poor man, and I wished him well.

Besides, what could he have said anyway?

Regardless, once he was gone, I missed his comforting presence. Suddenly, entirely alone, I felt sick-to-my-stomach again. Violently sick. Warily, I stood up from my chair, walked over to the wooden railing of the porch, fully expecting to vomit. Leaning over, I stared at the dark tinted windows of the still-waiting limousine, and I wondered if the driver was watching me. I shuddered several times, but nothing happened. Eventually it passed. Maybe, in time, the whole terrible afternoon would similarly pass away. I certainly hoped so.

I straightened up and stared at the lush green fields, the pleasant olive groves, and the little cemetery. I searched the landscape for the beautiful young Portuguese girl, but she wasn't there, and I was disappointed. I felt desperate. Alone, abandoned, and desolate. I felt like a man betrayed and abused.

Exactly how long I stood there looking for something that might bring me some kind of comfort, even distraction, I'm uncertain. It seemed to me like forever, as though it lasted for hours, but it was probably only fifteen minutes or so. The whole time, I stood right where I was on the porch and waited. I didn't know what else to do. Should I go back inside? Should I walk to the monastery? Or should I flee from this terrible place as quickly as I possibly could, and try to force the whole ugly business out of my disordered mind? I didn't know. I seemed incapable of making a decision.

For some reason, I remembered the little recorder that was still running inside my jacket pocket. I shut it off. I was tempted to drop it to the floor of the porch and crush it under my shoe, but I was distracted.

From nowhere, illogically, I noticed a powerful scent. It was the beautiful fragrance of roses. It seemed to come from nowhere in particular, but it was all around me and pervasive. It seemed to whirl gently around me and even, temporarily, it seemed to envelope me. It was a remarkable comfort. When it finally passed, I looked everywhere around me, but I couldn't find any roses.

Then I heard a slightly distracting sound from inside the cottage as the cardinal gradually emerged into the sunlight. He was visibly shaken, yet, at the same time, he was equally benumbed by everything that had happened.

"He's dead," he said simply, acknowledging my presence for the first time.

Again, I had no idea what to do. Or what to say. So we stood together in the hot afternoon in silence. Should I ask a question? Should I ask if my uncle had regained consciousness? Should I ask if there'd been a miraculous, last-minute regret or remorse? Or maybe I should ask the cardinal if my uncle was completely deranged, totally out of his mind? But I didn't ask anything. Probably because I didn't want to hear the answers, especially to the question about remorse.

I already knew the answer.

Barcelos turned and looked at me for the first time. He seemed, suddenly, to realize that he wasn't alone, and his natural compassion flashed through his personal desolation. Briefly. Even though he didn't actually say anything, I could sense the old man's concerns, and I greatly appreciated it.

The moment passed.

"I'll have them call you a cab," Barcelos said, rather flatly, in his accented English.

I nodded.

Then he stepped off the front porch, as his driver immediately popped out of the black limousine and opened the door to the back seat. When the doors were closed, the gleaming black car began to slowly make its way down the narrow stony path towards the monastery.

Abandoned once again, and completely dissatisfied, I walked over to the front door of the cottage and re-entered the deathroom. Oddly enough, the entire room was permeate with a lush scent of roses. Which made no sense. There were no flowers in the room. Maybe it was some kind of disinfectant, but it smelled remarkably real. Remarkably natural. It even, I'd have to admit, smelled rather lovely, so I pushed it from my mind.

Without thinking about what I was doing, I walked up to the bed and stared down at the cadaver, into the face of my dead uncle. It was a void. Blank. Expressionless, alien, and categorically inhuman. Surprisingly, I remained perfectly calm. I had no idea what I was doing, but I didn't care. I had no particular motive, and there was nothing I was intending to do, or say, or even think. I just stood there above the bed and stared down at the dead man's face, wishing that I'd never come to Portugal. Wishing that the Vatican had never called me last night. Wishing that I'd been left in peace.

In ignorance.

Unconsciously, I shifted my position and noticed something lying on the floor beneath my foot. Reflexively, I bent down and picked it up. It was a small piece of broken wood that had once been painted black. It looked like part of a small cross. Then I looked down at the corpse again. For some reason, I noticed that my uncle's left hand, beneath the sheet, seemed to be in a different position. Different from when I'd left the room earlier. Once again, without bothering to think, I acted impulsively. I pulled back the white sheet and saw the rest of the broken crucifix lying on the bed, lying in scattered pieces beside the desiccated corpse of my uncle.

Instinctively, I picked up the pieces.

This was the man's final sacrilege. Somehow, he'd conjured the strength to crush the little crucifix, the little Christ, within his dying hand, defacing the cross and everything it stood for. The sacrifice, the tragedy, and the promise of redemption.

"He hated those things."

Startled by the unexpected voice, I instantly jerked away from the exposed corpse. I felt a cold flush of adrenaline exploding within me and a frigid chill flashing down my spine.

It was the little boy.

He'd come back into the room again, using the back door. When I looked across the room, the child smiled. He obviously meant no harm, and his good-natured charming boyishness was a sudden and unexpected comfort.

I relaxed, returning the boy's smile.

I was surprised that he could speak English so well, but now, having heard him speak in a recognizable language, I understood his speech impediment. His verbal intonations had the distinctive mark of the deaf, but not the severely deaf.

He spoke again.

"Your taxi's coming soon."

"Thank you," I said, facing the boy directly, in case he needed to read my lips.

"You're to go to the National Library in Lisbon tomorrow morning and ask for António Zamora," he said, rather inexplicably, rather matter-of-factly.

I was taken aback.

"Who says so?" I asked, trying not to appear irritated.

"Father," the little boy answered, referring to the corpse on the bed.

I was disgusted.

After everything that I'd heard this afternoon, I found it impossible to still think of my dead uncle as a priest. I was also revulsed by the fact that the dead man was still attempting to communicate with the living, and that, in doing so, he was using an innocent little boy. But I said nothing. I didn't want to upset the child so I lifted up the bedsheet and carefully replaced it over the dead man's body. Maybe I should have covered his death-face as well.

I was ready to leave.

"Did you get your message?" the boy asked.

At first, I had no idea what he meant. Then I remembered the envelopes that I'd noticed earlier on the bedside table. I turned around and, sure enough, there was a single envelope remaining on top of the table. I picked it up. It had my name printed on the outside, but I had no inclination to read its contents. None. I was completely disgusted that the old man *still* wouldn't leave me alone, so I tucked the envelope into my back pants pocket.

Then I turned back to the little boy.

"What's your name?"

"Francisco."

I liked the name. Very much. It seemed to fit for some reason.

"I got one too," the boy confided, quite gratified by the idea, but I was confused.

"What do you mean?"

"A message," he said proudly.

I wasn't pleased in the least.

"You did?" I said with disinterest.

"I did," the boy assured me, obviously wanting to share his message, and I found it impossible to resist the little boy's charm.

"What did it say?" I asked reluctantly.

"*Submeta-se, outro guarda virá.*"

I smiled. The little boy naturally assumed that I could speak Portuguese.

"Very nice," I said.

The little boy repeated it.

"*Submeta-se, outro guarda virá.*"

It *was* very nice. Even though I couldn't comprehend its meaning, I appreciated its melodic sound, and the message rang in my head. It actually made me feel good for some reason, just as it seemed to make the little boy feel buoyant as well. I was amazed, given everything that had happened, that I could feel so perfectly comfortable in the little boy's presence.

Finally, I nodded toward the front door, and we left the room together. Out on the front porch, we stood beside each other, watching the distant black taxi making its careful way around the side of the monastery.

"Who was the priest?" I wondered out loud.

The boy seemed to know exactly who I meant.

"Gunther Raxx," he said flatly. "A Jesuit."

I thought it was rather odd that a polite little boy like Francisco didn't used the word "Father" when identifying a Roman Catholic priest.

The cab arrived.

"Take care of yourself, Francisco," I said, still grateful that the little boy had interrupted my personal hell with his charming good nature.

"*Sim*," the boy replied with a smile. "And may God bless you," he added, saying it so perfectly natural that I was greatly affected.

As my driver held the back door of the taxi open, I looked back at the little boy for the last time and smiled.

He smiled as well and waved.

"The library," he reminded gently.

Amazed, yet still confused, I settled back into the back seat and tried to push everything from my mind. I tried to think of Angelina. Which was extremely helpful. She alone was marvelous. Marvelously perfect. My *only* hope. As soon as we were together again, everything would be quickly forgotten.

But I remembered my message.

As the taxi cruised slowly past the monastery and onto the open roads of the Fatima countryside, I pulled the small envelope from my back pocket, opened it, and pulled out the little note inside. It was written in a distinctive handwriting, actually printed with a black fountain pen, which I recognized immediately, although it was obvious that the hand that had written the message was no longer as steady and firm as it had once been years ago. There was no letterhead, no salutation, no signature, just a single sentence:

Be worthy and Angelina will be your wife.

Chapter 6

Cabo da Roca

(Saturday, August 5th)

I wasn't sure *why* I was here, but I was here anyway.

It was 8:47 in the morning, and I was sitting in an isolated research room in the rare books wing of the Biblioteca Nacional, not far from the university in the north of Lisbon. I was waiting, patiently, for the reappearance of the curator, António Zamora, who didn't speak a word of English, who'd soon be returning with "something," most likely some books, which he'd obviously been instructed by "someone," most likely my uncle, to give to me.

And only me.

The dark wood-paneled room was actually quite comfortable, softly lit, and pleasantly cool, but I was still irritated at myself for being here. I should be flying back to Rome right now, but my curiosity had gotten the better of me. I tried to blame it on my reporter's instincts. And also on the little boy. If anyone else had relayed the message, I would have ignored it. But little Francisco was different, in all kinds of inexplicable ways, so I decided to do exactly what he'd asked me to do.

The door opened behind me.

António Zamora was thin and taciturn, a scholarly type, maybe fifty-five or so. Silently, he approached the room's huge wooden desk and carefully placed an antiquated leather-bound volume directly in front of me. Then he also set down three much newer books in a nearby pile. Leaning forward, he tapped twice on the oldest text with his forefinger.

I understood and nodded.

Then the librarian quietly retreated and left me alone in the room.

The rare book sitting in front of me was *Disputazioni Teologiche del secondo secolo*. Meaning *Theological Disputations of the Second Century*. It was written by Monsignor Eduardo Ricola, and it had been published in Rome in 1837. The fact that it was originally printed in Italian was, of course, fortunate for me, especially since there was probably never an English translation of such an obscure text. Protruding from the top of the book, there was a small slip of white paper, obviously marking the place where I was supposed to begin. Reflexively, I opened the book to the marker and read the page's heading:

"*Basilide.*"

I stopped.

I hesitated.

Did I really want to read this crap? Shouldn't I just get up and leave this place? Shouldn't I rush back to Rome as fast as I could? Into the arms of my love? The temptation to close the book and immediately leave for the airport was powerful, but I finally decided to read a bit. Why not? I was already here, maybe I should take a look?

Which I did.

The section on Basilides was only fifteen pages long, and I was hooked from the very first sentence. It was a summary-account of the life and thinking of the great Second Century heresiarch from Alexandria. Like most of the early Christian heretics, Basilides had obvious Eastern and gnostic roots. After all, didn't most of the more creatively impressive heresies emanate from the East? From places like Alexandria and Antioch, where the impulse for metaphysical speculation and extrapolation was apparently quite irresistible?

As for Basilides, he'd been markedly influenced by Zoroaster and the Parsees. He came to prominence during the reigns of the Emperors Hadrian and Antonius Pius, and he especially flourished between 120 and 140 A.D., becoming highly influential in lower Egypt, although his ideas would later migrate to Spain. Basilides claimed that he was receiving personal revelations from both St. Matthias, the thirteenth apostle, and from Glaucias, a disciple of St. Peter. He was quite prolific, writing his own gospel, *Evangelium Basilidis*; numerous odes and hymns; and a gospel commentary known as *Exegetics*. Nothing of his written work has survived, nor did the reputedly crushing refutation of his heresies by Agrippa Castor, but the heretical ideas of Basilides survived through a number of dismissive references and discussions in Irenaeus, Epiphanius, Hippolytus, and Clement of Alexandria.

His thinking was extremely creative, quite fantastic, and always engaging. He claimed that the great unborn-nameless-Father, known as Abrasax, first gave birth to Nous, then to Logos, and then to various other offspring, including the angels who created the 365 heavens, or spirit realms, from "matter," the fundamental principle of evil. The highest of the angels was the Yahweh-Jehovah-God of the Old

Testament, the monotheistic God of the Hebrews, who was opposed by all the other angels. Human life, like all other "matter," was fundamentally sinful, the physical manifestation of evil. In order to redeem such hopeless human creatures, Abrasax sent his first-born offspring Nous (Christ) to live among them. But, rather amazingly, the Passion itself never really happened. It was a fraud, a complete hoax, and the Basilidian Christ *never* suffered the ignominy of the cross, even though the souls of men were subsequently redeemed.

Thus Basilides' theology was a virtual compendium of heterodoxical thinking: it demeaned the creation; it demeaned Jehovah, it demeaned Christ; it rejected the Gospels; it denied the humanity of Christ; it repudiated Christ's miracles; it accepted both magic and sorcery; it disputed the resurrection of the body; and, most significantly, it denied the retributional Passion of Jesus Christ.

According to Basilides, it was *not* Christ who was crucified on the cross.

It was Simon of Cyrene!

Simon, of course, was the legendary cross-bearer, who'd been pressed into service by the Roman guard, and whose role in the Passion was described by Matthew, Mark, and Luke. According to Basilides, however, Simon was, in reality, Christ himself, under the "outward form" of the Cyrenian. He also claimed, most peculiarly, that Christ (in the form of Simon) actually laughed at the Roman executioners as he watched them crucify the Cyrenian. It's unclear in the Ricola text exactly why he did so, and I assumed that the explanation for the laughter has never survived from the Second Century.

This was the dramatic fanciful heresy that had strongly attracted my uncle in his own heretical meanderings.

When I finished the Ricola text, I shut the book and stared across the room. I didn't know what to think, or even what I was *supposed* to think about something so perfectly ludicrous. But I had to admit, I was intrigued, so I decided to press on.

I reached over, grabbed the other three books, and slid them in front of me. All of them were works by Fr. Bernardi Sorel (obviously a pseudonym used by my uncle), all of them in English translation: *The Human Christ*; *The Cyrene*; and a brand-new copy of *Rennes-le-Château: The Mystery of Christ*. Without hesitation, I opened *The Cyrene* and began reading. I didn't stop until the text ended 325 pages later. It was absolutely amazing. It was also absolutely sickening. Not only because of its outrageous heresy, but because, even worse, of the remarkable subtlety of its deceit.

The first section of the book was an alluring and admiring encomium to the charity and the humanity of Jesus Christ. In the second section, Sorel cleverly, seductively, began making the case that given the human-Christ's "near-perfection," it would be both unfair and illogical to assume that he could, or should, suffer inordinately. Besides, his extraordinary charity and kindness were more than enough to salvage the pathetic human race and fully redeem it. Finally, in the amazing third and concluding section of the book, Sorel suggests, rather convincingly, that Simon the Cyrene was crucified at Calgary as a "stand-in" for Christ, as a symbol of Christ's merciful and sacrificial nature.

The book also asserts that only Peter and his brother Andrew, who supposedly wrote the fourth gospel (St. John's gospel), knew what was happening, and that they both approved, believing that Christ should never suffer a humiliation and disgrace like Golgotha. At the book's conclusion, Sorel was rather vague about what happened to the post-Ascension Christ. The Ascension, of course, was another well-intentioned deception, and Sorel alludes to the possibility that Christ travelled north into modern-day Europe. The obvious implication is that the rest of the story would be discussed in a forthcoming book.

When I was finished, I sat back in my chair and marveled at my uncle's unlimited propensity for evil. I felt personally violated. I felt sick and hollow within. I knew that the book, a bestseller in several European countries, must have sown the seeds of doubt in the minds of many of its readers. It was, in its subtle presentation, an absolute masterpiece of deception and seduction. It was easy-to-read, yet never condescending. It was simultaneously reasonable and alluring, supported by a plethora of scholarly research. Surely this book had damaged many lives. After all, who wouldn't be fascinated by such a book?

Who wouldn't be affected in one way or another?

For a long time, I sat in the silent library room and stared at the book. Even its cover was striking: a bright-red slightly tilted cross on a white background. Eventually, almost impulsively, I opened the book again and carefully reread its short preface, which made several unexplained references to Rennes-le-Château. Then I noticed that the preface was dated just a few months before the book's copyright date, and that it ended with the author's name, actually his pen name, "Fr. Bernardi Sorel," and his location at the time, Lisbon, Portugal.

Something was wrong!

I was stunned!

I stared rather stupidly at the word "Lisbon." Was it possible? Suddenly, everything that had happened during the past thirty-six hours was turned upside down. Completely upside down. And even though I refused to allow myself too much hope, I knew that I'd have to find out for myself, and there was only one way to do it.

Immediately, I rose from my chair, left the library, and took a taxi to the cardinal's residence in southwest Lisbon, not far from Jerónimos Monastery. Outside the cardinal's palatial residence, there was a sizable milling crowd of people, obviously reporters, all babbling among themselves in Portuguese. Since the front doors of the building were inexplicably locked, I surreptitiously slipped around the side of the building, climbed over a hedge, and entered the back of the residence. Then I walked up a flight of stairs and made my way down a long deserted corridor toward the main entrance.

The young man sitting at the front desk was obviously astonished when I appeared from nowhere, but he was still polite, if perfunctory.

"I was with the cardinal yesterday," I explained. "I'm certain that he'll want to see me."

He was naturally suspicious.

"I'm afraid the cardinal won't be seeing anyone today," he explained in a rather passable English, although he seemed oddly distracted.

As if uneasy.

Uncertain.

"Are you a reporter?"

"Yes," I said, a bit too quickly, a bit too honestly, "but this is a personal matter."

He seemed horrified.

"It's impossible!" he said, attempting to put an end to everything. "You'll have to leave immediately!"

I didn't budge.

"I'm not leaving until you call the cardinal and ask him if he wants to see me."

The young man was equally adamant, and he waved for a uniformed guard at the door.

Across the room, an older priest, maybe sixty or so, was observing the disturbance, and he walked over to assist the young receptionist.

I spoke first.

"I'm the nephew of Fr. Bryce Sinclair."

Instantly, the priest stopped where he was and listened.

"I was with Cardinal Barcelos yesterday in Fatima," I explained, "and I need to see him again. I'm absolutely positive that he'll want to see me. Immediately."

The old priest thought it over a moment, then he looked at me intently.

"It has nothing to do with the allegations?"

Allegations?

"*What* allegations? I have no idea what you're talking about," I assured the old man.

Convinced, he picked up the desk phone, waited a moment, spoke briefly in Portuguese, then put down the receiver.

"Come with me, young man."

Very quickly, I was led upstairs, then down a longish corridor to the far end of the building. When the priest knocked on the huge wooden doors, a muffled voice could be heard from within. When the priest opened one of the doors, I stepped inside the room. As I did so, the door shut behind me.

Unexpectedly, I was now standing in the cardinal's sleeping quarters. It was a large room, bright and rather luxurious, meticulously decorated with handsome antiques, lush carpets, fine curtains, and elaborate light fixtures, as well as numerous oils, both sacred and profane. It was a remarkable contrast to the bare, spartan, blank-white walls of my uncle's tiny cottage-cell in Fatima.

Sitting within a comfortable antique chair, in complete disarray, was Cardinal Barcelos. He was drinking some kind of liquor, and it was perfectly obvious that he'd already had too much to drink.

I didn't care.

I wasn't here to waste my time.

"What happened yesterday?" I demanded.

The cardinal glanced at me, as if recognizing me for the first time. He actually seemed relieved, but only momentarily. He looked like a man whose entire life had suddenly collapsed around him. He was a mess. He was pathetic, and he knew it. It suddenly dawned on me that maybe the true authorship of the "Sorel" books had somehow gone public this morning with the release of *Rennes-le-Château*. Which would certainly explain all the reporters outside and the cardinal's present condition.

He answered my question with another question.

"Don't you know?"

"No, I don't know," I assured him.

"It was all done to wake me up," he explained as he took another drink of what seemed to be a dark wine or a dark liqueur.

"Did it?"

"It certainly did. Look at me!"

I did as I was told. I took a long and serious look at the old man, who seemed eerily inert, defeated, and completely self-absorbed.

Maybe even despairing.

Maybe that's appropriate, I thought to himself.

"Have you seen the morning papers?" he asked.

"No, I haven't."

The cardinal pointed over at his unmade bed. There was a copy of Lisbon's *Diario*. I picked it up.

The headline was huge:

"CARDIAL BARCELOS ACUSADO!"

Instantly, I scanned through the first paragraph looking for Latinates. Then I saw the word "*sexualidade*." I was initially stunned, and yet I suppose I shouldn't have been surprised at all. The cardinal had, apparently, been accused of some kind of sexual misconduct.

"What *kind* of sex scandal?" I demanded, turning back to Barcelos.

The cardinal took no offense at my obvious aggression, my obvious condemnation. He was too psychologically debilitated to care, but he did answer the question quite clearly.

"A young girl has accused me of seducing her," he said rather flatly.

"*How* young?"

"Fourteen," the Bishop of Lisbon replied with a rather disturbing resignation.

I was repulsed.

"That's disgusting."

When the cardinal made no response, I couldn't help adding, with scathing sarcasm, "I thought you only used prostitutes?"

The helpless cardinal looked at me with total confusion in his eyes, as if from another world.

"I have *many* sins to answer for, young man, but not *that*. Never. I *never* touched the girl. I don't even know who she is. It's a penance, don't you understand that?"

Yes, I *did* understand.

The renegade cardinal, the *true* author of *The Cyrene* and the other heretical books by "Fr. Bernardi Sorel," had been called, yesterday afternoon, to the bedside of his one-time friend to be shamed into changing his despicable life. Maybe that was why the Jesuit was also there, to make certain that the cardinal's shame and all of my uncle's revelations were, in some sense, made public. Maybe my uncle had been exactly right in doing what he'd done, even though I'd foolishly misinterpreted everything, because the desolate man sitting in front of me no longer seemed like a brazen self-confident heretic. He'd been completely crushed and defeated. Even talking about penance. Maybe there *was* a glimmer of hope. Maybe I should try to find a modicum of compassion for such a pathetic monster.

Maybe he *really* could repent.

On the other hand, I wasn't fully certain if I should believe what I was seeing. Maybe it was just a momentary lapse, a passing weakness, a temporary break in the man's all-consuming vanity, incited by the sudden horror of losing his position, his power, his luxuries. Maybe even his sports car and his beachhouse.

Regardless, I still wanted to be perfectly clear about everything that had taken place yesterday in Fatima.

"So my uncle did what he did just to shake you up?" I asked directly.

"Yes, and Fr. Raxx as well, and you too, I suppose."

Which raised another good point.

"What was I doing there anyway?"

"I have no idea. Maybe so you'd show up here today and further chastise me. In Father's place."

Was it possible?

I wondered.

Then the man who might-have-been-pope looked up, into my eyes, with remarkable sincerity.

"He was a prophet. Did you know that?"

I had no idea, and I had no idea how to respond.

"He categorically believed in miracles," Barcelos continued, "and he associated with various miracle-workers. He even performed them himself. The miraculous happened all around him, in fact. Especially during his more recent years in Fatima."

"I didn't know," I admitted, uncertain what to think.

But the cardinal had already collapsed back into his overwhelming desolation and desperation, slumping down into his chair. Nevertheless, I still found it hard to pity the man, but I did wonder about my uncle, especially about his four final "prophesies."

Someone, he'd said, quite clearly, was going to hell.

I decided not to think about it. After all, I didn't believe in hell anyway, or *any* of those Catholic mythologies. I walked over to the little table near the devastated bishop, took the man's glass and his near-empty bottle of Port, and walked into the nearby bathroom. Then I dumped the liquids into the sink.

When I was finished, I returned to the bedroom and noticed that the cardinal was alert once again, seemingly unconcerned about his missing Port.

"What do you do now?" I asked.

"Resign," he said without hesitation. "Then wait."

"Wait for what?" I wondered.

The cardinal shrugged. He didn't know himself.

"Forgiveness?" he suggested. "Maybe even, if I'm fortunate, absolution."

Maybe there *was* some hope.

Maybe my uncle had been right.

Then I noticed the little envelope lying in Barcelos's lap.

"What's that?" I asked, even though I knew exactly what it was.

"Here," he said, lifting up the letter

I took it.

"Should I read it?"

"Of course," he said. "Maybe you're *supposed* to read it."

"Is it in English?"

"Yes."

I still hesitated.

"Better yet," Barcelos decided, "take it with you. I'm not likely to forget it."

I nodded my agreement, then tucked the little envelope into my jacket pocket.

"Did my uncle have a good confession?" I asked, changing the subject, still hoping to put my mind at rest.

"Yes," the cardinal remembered, "right after you and Fr. Raxx left the room. It was a model confession, in fact, made to the most unworthy of confessors."

I was encouraged by the cardinal's new-found self-awareness. Maybe he could, somehow, someway, as my uncle had hoped, find a way to rectify himself.

"The man was a saint," Barcelos summed up. "Even at the moment of his death, he was thinking of others."

I nodded.

I was extremely grateful for everything that the cardinal, now trapped in his own interminable miseries, had decided to tell me. His assurance that my uncle had *not* been a heretic, and that he'd lived and died a decent man and priest, was powerfully comforting, despite everything that I'd suffered yesterday in Fatima and even today in Lisbon.

"What am I supposed to do?" I asked the troubled cardinal.

"Learn something, I suppose."

It was the best he could offer, but it was enough for right now. Maybe it was more than enough.

It was time to leave.

"Are you all right?" I asked, meaning, "Are you all right to be left alone?"

He understood my meaning.

"Yes."

I walked to the door, then hesitated.

"Who's Fr. Raxx?" I wondered out loud.

"One of my advisors."

"Where is he now?" I asked, thinking that surely he should be helping the cardinal in his time of difficulty.

"He's gone," the old man explained. "He left for Lyon early this morning. He had some bad news of his own today."

I was tempted to ask about the bad news, but I didn't bother. Instead, I opened the door.

"Pray for me," a troubled voice called out from behind me.

But I never pray anymore.

So I said nothing, leaving the room in silence.

Outside, on the streets of Belém, a lovely evening had fallen over the city. Lisbon gleamed rather majestically in the comfortable twilight and the occasional brisk breezes from the nearby Tagus were particularly refreshing. But within my mind and heart, there was nothing but irresolution and confusion. I felt as though something uncertain had been initiated in my life, and I felt as though it was still unresolved. I was deeply discontent, and I knew, without doubt, that I wasn't ready to fly home to Angelina.

Not yet.

I sat in a small café near Rua Bartolomeu Dias and readjusted my flight schedule for the second time today. Then I called my love. She didn't answer, and, in a way, I was grateful. I didn't feel that I could adequately express myself right now, so I was glad to leave her a brief message. Something about obligations and unforeseen delays, about how much I loved her and wished to be within her arms again.

Which was all true.

I took the train to Cascais on the coast and hired a taxi driver to take me thirteen miles northwest to Cabo da Roca, the westernmost point of the European continent, which thrust out over the wild Atlantic. By the time I arrived, an approaching storm was apparent, although not quite visible. I could feel it silently creating itself in the distant cool night air, and I didn't mind at all. I was glad, in fact. Without hesitation, I walked over to the edge of the cliff, not far from the lighthouse, not far from the little cross monument inscribed with the famous line from Camões, the greatest of all Portuguese poets:

"Onde a terra se acaba e o mar começa."

Apparently meaning:

Where the land ends and the sea begins.

I sat down on the granite cape.

The protruding cliff was high above the Atlantic, more than a hundred feet above the ever-raging, ever-frothing, endlessly-churning sea. The ocean. Tonight, given the coming storm, the cape was entirely deserted, and I was both pleased and unsurprised. There was something a bit too wild, a bit too bleak, about this desolate place. It was harsh and eerily remote. It was also, of course, marvelously beautiful, but it still had that rather unspeakable intimation of death. Which I didn't mind at all. I've always loved, even obsessed, about the Atlantic Ocean, always accepting its undeniable undercurrents of death and mortality.

I stared out over the dark, violent, gradually storming Atlantic. My home in Maryland was 3,500 miles away, far across the seductively deadly waters. Both of my parents were still there. Now. Together. Maybe even my sister was with them, or maybe she was off with Richard, her fiancé, whom I barely knew but liked quite a bit.

Above everything, of course, was the moon, the elusive goddess, ducking in and out of the gray-black night-clouds, driven by furiously erratic winds. Intermittently, she would flash down her silver glints on the chaotic white-capped waves below. She was almost full tonight, and tomorrow night she'd dramatically eclipse herself before a watching world, and I would watch her vanish into the blackness with Angelina beside me.

It would be perfect.

But tonight I wanted to be alone. Alone with the waves and the moon, the two things that had always given me comfort in my youth. Throughout my entire life. As a boy, I'd been so enamored of the power of the ocean, especially the mysterious motions of its waves, that I seriously thought about becoming an oceanographer of some kind. For years, I read every available book about the great movements of the sea, its tides, its currents, its waves. I learned that every single wave, like every single snowflake, is unique and beautiful in its own special way. I studied all the appropriate descriptive terms and all the requisite science: the crest, the trough, the wavelength, the period, the frequency, the swell, the density, the wind stress, and the surface tension. I was delighted to discover that even in today's modern world, the complex actions of the oceans are still not fully comprehended by scientists, whose attempts to accurately predict the erratic behavior of the oceans, though much improved, were only moderately successful.

I came to comprehend the oceans as vast reservoirs of potential energy. It was Aristotle, unsurprisingly, who made the first crucial observations about the interaction of the wind on the water. That the whole surface of the ocean was actually a fantastically subtle interface of energy lying between two gigantic fluid and congruent systems, the air above and the water below. Where there was *always* frictional, energy-creating stress between the two conflicting layers. Where the waves, in consequence, transported the resultant energy. Thus the sea was never at rest. *Never.* Almost anything could happen in the wildly unpredictable oceans of the world.

Oddly enough, nothing I learned, not even the technical stuff, diminished my aesthetic appreciation for the ocean. Nor did it mitigate the magic of my solitary nights, almost every night, watching the rough Atlantic agitate off the Maryland coast at Ocean City. Nevertheless, I eventually decided against pursuing the ocean as a vocation. As a career. I decided that I didn't want to spend the rest of my life examining the sea. I felt that I already knew enough. Maybe too much. Instead, I wanted to spend the rest of my life enjoying the ocean, which I've done, whenever I'm able. Like tonight. Because it was always a comfort, no matter how cruel, how stark, how desolate it might seem to others. The sea, like the moon, was my companion.

My friend.

Tonight, the frigid waves below me would occasionally smash against the cliff walls so violently that the sea spray would rise up into the night and filter down, over me, softly, in a light mist. I didn't mind at all. I was exactly where I wanted to be. Before me lay the storming surface of the ocean, where the sharp night breezes were ploughing long streaks of white foam. The waves were high tonight, steep and angry. Intermittently, their churning surfaces glimmered with the silverish light-flashes of the moon.

Most human cultures invariably recognize moonlight, reflecting on the waters below, as a symbol of beauty, virtue, and love. Often divine love. The Chinese believe that the goddess of the moon becomes distressed if her reflection on the water is disturbed. On a lake. Or a pond. Especially if the disturbance is caused by something human. But, of course, the reflection of the moon across the great oceans of the world is *always* distorted, even on the calmest days, and I'm convinced that the moon-goddess wouldn't mind at all. That she'd fully appreciate the turbulent power of the sea, which she so much affected. That she'd enjoy the endlessly fantastic play of her silver lights across the agitated surface.

I certainly did.

Once again, I'd come to the violent sea, as I'd always done when I was a young boy, to calm my troubled soul. I was certain that something had changed or altered in my life, even though I couldn't fully comprehend it. Or express it. I was certain that something had happened, and I knew that I needed to be alone. Despite all the roller-coaster anxieties of the past two days, I didn't *feel* that much different, just tired and confused. Which was perfectly natural. But I still had the sense that I was now different in some fundamental way. That I'd been forced to recognize that there are deeper more significant things in life, within my own life. Things that I've been running away from, which I now felt I could no longer avoid. My curiosity had been reinvigorated, and my personal depthlessness was painfully apparent. I'd become lazy and frivolous and shallow, and now I wanted more from life, and now I'd have to seek it out.

It wasn't, however, any kind of conversion. Definitely not. There wasn't anything religious about it at all. I was absolutely certain about that. It was simply a realization that I'd been avoiding the more serious and permanent things in life, in human existence, which I definitely didn't see as a matter of religion. I saw such things as a matter of personal ethics. I wanted, as my uncle had expressed it, to be "worthy." I wished to better myself for Angelina's sake, and I was determined to live my life less on the surface of things. I wasn't, of course, ruling out the "fun" in life, or the "good times," but I wanted a life of more substance, more "worth." I didn't want to be a shallow man. What's wrong with that? I wanted to give Angelina much more than I was giving her now. In truth, I wanted to give her everything.

Yes, everything.

It was, I realized, a renewed and rather profound sense that I needed to think more deeply and learn a whole lot more. To become more responsible. In the end, I fully expected that none of these things would alter me or my life substantially, but they would definitely make me more deserving of Angelina's love. Whatever I might learn or discover, I was certain that it would lead me back to the most fundamental conception of virtue. To love. To Angelina herself. Amazingly, I now appreciated her even more than I had before, which would have seemed impossible just forty-eight hours ago. Didn't I already worship the ground she walked on? Of course, I did. But it wasn't enough. She was so much more virtuous than I'd ever comprehended before, and I resolved to make myself into someone who fully deserved to be her husband, to be her friend, to be her lover.

A tremendous blast suddenly cracked beneath me, and a wide sheet of the frigid Atlantic rose up into the night before me. Almost instantly, it dissipated into the darkness and fell over me like a gentle rain. I loved it, and I laughed out loud. I felt like calling out to the ocean, "Do it again!" My previously troubled mind was now comfortably content and calm. The ocean, the moon, and the dark of night had flushed away the detritus of the past two days: the false confession, the death of my uncle, the perversities of Barcelos, and the sulfuric stink of the heretics. Now I could go back home. Now I could finally go back to Rome and see my love again.

I wished for nothing else in the whole wide world.

Then, just before I stood up to leave, I remembered the envelope that was still tucked inside my jacket pocket. My uncle's message to Barcelos. Should I bother to read it? What difference did it make? But why not? I took it out and opened it up. It was soaked with the dampness of the sea-spray, and I had a little trouble reading it in the inconsistent moonlight. Since it made no discernible sense, I put it away and quickly forgot about it:

Before Rome, St. Gerard.

Chapter 7

Isola Tiberina

(Sunday, August 6th)

Where did everything go wrong?

Where *exactly*?

Was it foolishly believing that my uncle was a heretic? Which was a betrayal, an unconscionable lack of faith in someone I loved. Or was it reading all those blasphemous heretical texts? There's no denying, no matter how much they revulsed me, that all their clever perversities simultaneously attracted and intrigued me. Or was it sitting on Cabo da Roca, staring into the raging ocean, believing, regardless of everything that had happened, that things would be pretty much the same again. That everything would be all right?

Maybe.

Maybe not.

Three hours after I landed at Fiumicino, I met Angelina at the elegant San Teodora on Via dei Fienili behind the Roman Forum. It's always been our favorite restaurant in the city, and Angelina was just as excited to see me as I was to see her. It seemed as though we'd been separated for months. As always, she was stunning, in a short, chic, yellow dress, maybe Valentino, that I'd never seen before. She looked spectacular, radiant. I thought my love should be cited in all the travel books: "Forget the Forum, forget the Coliseum, visit San Teodora on Sunday night and hope you'll catch a glimpse of the Roman goddess, Angelina Parenzo."

As for me, I was finally wearing fresh clothes again: a rather sleek, off-white Armani suit with besom pockets, over a snug navy-blue Battistoni with a silver collar bar. Angelina looked me up-and-down, smiled, and said, "You must be the handsomest man in Rome." Even though I knew it wasn't true, I felt like it was.

As we sat together at an outside table, not far from Campidoglio and the theater of Marcellus, her lovely, thickish-longish hair glistened in the soft floodlights, as did her red moist lips. Which I'd kissed outside the restaurant the moment we met. She seemed eager and passionate throughout the meal, and I was thinking about doing it again. All the difficulties of the past few days were completely forgotten. I was back with my perfect lover in the marvelously exhilarating city that we both adored.

Nothing else mattered.

As usual, she had the famous fried artichokes, and I tried the *tonnarelli cacio e pepe*. Everything was perfect. Everything was exquisite. We spoke with intimacy, just like the young lovers we were, with meaningful looks, with meaningful lovers' laughs, and we were perfectly content.

As for the canceled trip to Cannes, she couldn't have cared less:

"We can go to the beach anytime," she said, dismissing the whole thing. "Besides, I'd rather watch the little moon do her tricks right here in Rome. After all, Rome's the most romantic place in the whole world. Right?"

I looked at her face, into her seductively dark eyes.

"It certainly is."

I meant it.

Besides, Angelina was already thinking about making a trip to Paris next month for one of the big fashion shows, and she wanted me to come along.

"Won't you come with me, love?" she asked, breathlessly, with all her excited talk about Paris.

"Of course. I've heard Paris is also a fairly romantic city."

She smiled.

She liked the idea.

As a matter of fact, she seemed to like everything tonight, especially when I hinted about my forthcoming proposal, our forthcoming engagement. As always, it gave me tremendous pleasure to see Angelina's pleasures.

Finally, during dessert, she began to ask about the details and specifics of my trip to Portugal. She was completely fascinated. After all, not everyone's boyfriend gets sent off to Fatima by the Vatican. By the pope. So I told her everything, and she was spellbound. She was also spooked, intrigued, and amazed. Watching her wide range of reactions convinced me that the whole thing had probably been worth it.

"Why didn't your uncle let you know what was going on?" she asked, quite logically.

"I don't know. Maybe he intended to, but I got there too late. Or maybe he thought I'd have enough sense to know better. That I'd have enough faith in the man, and everything that he'd ever stood for, and that I'd realize it was just a ruse of some kind."

"Maybe he was trying to force you to think about things?" she wondered out loud.

"Maybe, he did. I really don't know. I guess I'll never know."

Later, we walked west to the Tiber, then strolled over Ponte Fabricio, the oldest bridge in Rome, towards Isola Tiberina, one of Angelina's favorite places in the ancient city. Even as a child visiting her Italian cousins in Rome, she was always attracted to the picturesque little island that sat in the midst of the legendary river, being, supposedly, the exact spot where the she-wolf found Romulus and Remus. It was also the city's legendary site for "cures" and "healings." My love loved strolling beneath the island's tall pines, beside the flowing waters, beneath the belltower of the Tenth Century church of San Bartolomeo, which allegedly held the remains of the martyred apostle St. Bartholomew.

Both of us were fully aware of Isola Tiberina's odd and ancient history. We both knew that during a devastating plague in the Third Century B.C., a Roman delegation had been sent to Epidaurus in Greece to visit the Sibyl for guidance. When they were instructed to build a temple to Aesculapius, the son of Apollo, the god of healing, they dutifully agreed and quickly returned back home. Finally, sailing up the Tiber, they saw, to their astonishment, a gigantic serpent slither off their ship and swim to the small island and vanish. Naturally, they assumed that this was a sign from the gods that they should build their temple to Aesculapius on the little island. Which they did. Subsequently, for over two thousand years, the island has always been associated with healing, restoration, and recuperation. Even today, at the west end of the island, the Franciscans continued the ancient tradition by maintaining the Hospital of Fatebenefratelli, which was apparently built on the site of a medieval hospital.

So the little island was not only lovely, especially at night, but it was also full of fascinating history. But *most* important, it was beloved by my Angelina. This would be the perfect place to watch the night's eclipse. Certainly better than some faddish beach in southern France.

Of course, we weren't the only ones in Rome who knew what was happening in the darkened skies tonight, and the Isola was a bit more crowded than usual, but everything was still pleasant and relaxing. Eventually, rather leisurely, we strolled to the east end of the island near San Bartolomeo, stopping in the same secluded place where we'd stopped on many other Roman nights, where I held Angelina in my arms, closely, as she held me closely as well, gently kissing my neck.

And yet, there was something on her mind.

Something she was curious about.

"What did you do last night?"

"I went to Cabo da Roca. On the Atlantic coast."

She was surprised.

"Why?"

"To think about things," I said, not trying to be either vague or elusive.

"About what?" she pressed.

I really didn't know, so I shrugged my shoulders.

"About everything, I guess."

Which was unsatisfactory.

There was a momentary pause.

"I see," she said.

And that was that.

At that precise *exact* moment, everything went wrong. When my Angelina simply said, "I see." Those two little words. Two simple words. Maybe I sensed it in her voice, but I refused to acknowledge it. Maybe, in some way, I sensed her sudden apprehension. Her disappointment. Her intuitive understanding that some kind of change had occurred in her lover. A change she could never accept.

Did Angelina, herself, realize that it was the beginning of the end?

Probably not.

I certainly didn't.

But it was.

Without a doubt.

Something had changed in her perfectly comfortable world, and she sensed it without fully comprehending it. Suddenly, there was an undesirable intrusion into her orderly life, and she definitely didn't want to deal with it. She wanted things to remain exactly as they were.

Forever.

But her lover had gone off to Portugal for two short days, and he'd come back different. He'd come back needing something, something that was still rather vague, but something that was definitely different from her. Something that was even *more* than her. Because now, beneath the surface of our lives, underneath the superficial status quo, there was some kind of intrusive craving, some kind of new seriousness, and she wanted no part of it. She didn't want it anywhere near her, and she certainly didn't want it hanging over our life together. Somehow Angelina apprehended, without the slightest doubt, that it would change us both, irrevocably, whether we wanted it to or not.

And she wasn't comfortable with it.

She wasn't amenable to any new or additional priorities insinuating into our lives. Certainly not new restrictions. She was already perfectly decent, perfectly virtuous, without the trappings of religion, and she'd been that way her whole life. She expected, even demanded, exactly the same from me. But now I'd gone off to some backward country with a bunch of bizarre priests and come back to her damaged.

Altered.

Yet, at that particular moment, at the east end of Isola Tiberina, the moment passed us by almost instantly. As if nothing had happened. As if imperceptible. Then arm in arm, we found an isolated bench near the river and sat down together in the Roman night. Where we held each other closely, as she rested her head, tenderly, against my shoulder, as we looked up at the sky together.

It was time.

The lovely moon grew dim.

Subtly, she began to change her colors, from lovely greens to soft reds to flaming yellows, gradually moving herself into the dark shadow cast by the planet earth, into the distant voids of space. Slowly, extremely slowly, she slipped into the earth's dark umbra which began to swallow her up. But not quite. Because a minimal bit of sunlight had somehow refracted itself off the earth's atmosphere, leaving the moon ever-so-faintly lit within its umbra. Then, gradually, the Queen of the Night vanished into the blackness, as all around her, the starry diamonds of the sky, gleamed forth, all-the-more brightly, as if deeply agitated, as if concerned about the fate of the missing moon, as if searching for their lost companion. It was very beautiful. Never as garish, or even as rare, as an eclipse of the sun, but, in its own way, more lovely, more mysterious, more romantic.

In ancient cultures, as with the Egyptians, lunar eclipses were envisioned as portents of catastrophe. Within the tribes of Israel, they were recognized as telling signs of divine discontent, anger, and forthcoming judgment. The ancient Incas imagined that the moon was actually being devoured, slowly dying, and other cultures believed that she was hiding herself because she was angry with mankind. Still others felt that she was being seduced by the sun, and even the thoughtful Greeks, whose Thales had been the first to accurately predict the eclipses of the moon, were eerily spooked by the vanishings of the moon, which had a particularly precipitous consequence in 413 B.C. during the Peloponnesian War.

Under Nicias, the Athenians had foolishly invaded Sicily. From the start, the campaign was a disaster, so Nicias planned for an immediate evacuation from the island, but the moon suddenly vanished from the sky. Which the Athenian soothsayers assumed was a warning *not* to withdraw. So Nicias was ordered to stay right where he was. "For thrice nine days." So he did as he was told. Almost immediately, Gylippus, the Spartan commander, destroyed the Athenian fleet and blockaded the harbor. In time, he was able to wipe out the entire Athenian army, including Nicias, in the greatest military disaster in Greek history.

So much for reading the intentions of the moon.

Yes, it's true, I know lots of stuff about the moon, maybe too much, but I said nothing tonight, sitting with my love in silence. Intertwined, in the moonlessness, as we watched together, for nearly two hours, until the resurrected silver satellite finally, slowly, re-emerged, as a sign of hope, a sign of beauty. What had been briefly lost, now was found. What had once seemed lost, was now returned. Occasionally, intimately, beneath the rare celestial phenomenon, we'd kiss each other tenderly and speak of love, of contentment, with all the eager passions of passionate young lovers. Impervious to lunar portents.

Impervious also to the terrible traumas of the lovely moon herself, who, when she first entered the earth's umbra, was swept by a frigid wave of deadly cold which dropped her temperature 270 degrees in less than an hour.

Then back again.

In the weeks that followed, everything, quickly, almost inexplicably, went downhill. At first, of course, I ignored the signs, believing that I was seeing things that weren't really there. But eventually they became too obvious to ignore. Even on the day following the eclipse, there'd been a certain distance in Angelina's demeanor, an unprecedented wariness. Within two days, I was hearing her say things that she would have *never* said before in those two wonderful years since we'd met at Giolitti's: "I need to get home early tonight, Bryce." The next night, when I held her close, she whispered that she wasn't "feeling just right tonight." By the following weekend, I was hearing the impossible: "I'm sorry, Bryce, but I can't make it tonight."

I was also, I was certain, being cut out of her trip to Paris. She was still planning to go, but she never mentioned it again. Not once.

I wasn't entirely stupid. I knew what was going on, but I didn't want to face it. I became uncharacteristically edgy and obsessive. I worried all the time, and my work suffered. Everything suffered. Everything seemed to be happening at breakneck speed.

Finally, desperately, I decided to do something about it. I went over to Buccellati's on Via Condotti and brought her a colorless diamond. A hundred points, VS1 clarity, with a Tiffany setting. It wiped me out, but I didn't care. I didn't even think about it. All I cared about was whether she'd like it, and whether she'd think it was beautiful, and whether she'd say "yes."

I decided to give it to her that night.

She called.

It was late afternoon, and I was sitting in my office at the *Herald* thinking about what I would say later that evening. But as soon as I picked up the phone, as soon as I heard her voice, I sensed impending disaster.

"This is hard to say, Bryce," she began, obviously struggling.

I said nothing, waiting for the inevitable.

"I think we need to slow down."

I could hear the sadness in her voice. As well as the resolve.

My heart imploded in my chest. I felt dazed, lightheaded, breathless.

I tried to recover. I tried to get her to talk about it. When that failed, I pressed her to meet with me tonight, anywhere, but she hesitated. But I was relentless. Finally, she gave in.

"Meet me at the fountain at six."

"I'll be there," I said, as she cut off at the other end.

Before six, I arrived at Trevi Fountain with the ring in my pocket. The cramped little piazza was packed with tourists, and I felt certain that Angelina had chosen the place for exactly that reason. There was nothing that was private or intimate about the Trevi tonight. It was jammed with hordes of milling tourists, all throwing coins over their shoulders, taking photos of Salvi's Neptune and the stupid Tritons and their stupid horses, maybe dreaming of *La dolce vita,* imagining Anita Ekberg sloshing around in the ever-churning waters of the fountain.

This was surely the worst place in Rome to meet with your love and try to stave off a break-up. Resigned, weary, I sat down on the edge of the fountain, beneath all the dramatic baroque excess, and listened mindlessly to the bubbling waters rushing from Agua Virgo.

Suddenly, Angelina was there, standing above me. I looked up. She was wearing green tonight. She was lovelier than anything I'd ever seen in my entire life. I stood up, and we talked. It was surprisingly calm, even rational, and Angelina was characteristically kind and gentle, but it was over. Finished. She'd made up her mind, and there was no turning back. No matter how much it hurt. Shamelessly, I begged her to give me another chance.

But she was adamant.

I begged her to tell me "why?"

"Because you've changed," she said with certitude.

"But how?"

"You just have," she said rather evasively.

"But *how*?" I pressed her.

"You know as well as I do, Bryce," she said, slightly irritated.

But I *didn't* know, and she never really clarified things. Maybe because she couldn't. Then it was over.

She was gone.

She walked away, vanishing into the crowd, as I entered the portals of a desperate hell.

The subsequent months, the subsequent two years, were nothing less than a prolonged excruciating torment. The low point, or, at least, the most flagrantly humiliating moment, occurred a week after the Trevi Fountain when I hid myself across the street from Parenzo's, Angelina's boutique on the fashionable Via Borgognona, then followed her over to the Spanish Steps. It's a truism that most of the Romans leave Scalinata and Piazza di Spagna for the tourists, but Angelina was quite different. She loved the place. She loved its peculiar palm trees, its 138 travertine steps, and the lofty Trinta dei Monti with its double bell towers. She believed that the Steps were the beating heart of Rome itself, and she ate her lunch there every single Thursday afternoon, often alone, sometimes with friends.

That day, she was alone.

She sat with her little lunch in the bright Roman sunshine, in a dark red dress, wearing large black sunglasses, and looking very much like an Italian movie starlet, attracting, as always, as many stares as the surrounding Roman monuments. I didn't care. I never blamed the starers. Why shouldn't they stare? For a few moments, I sat there unnoticed and did the same thing myself.

Staring at Angelina.

Finally, I stood up and walked over. She was sitting beneath the Keats House where the poet had died in 1821. She always loved Keats, especially his final poem, "Bright Star, Would I Were Stedfast."

I walked up to my love, knelt down, and proposed. Immediately, a little crowd of enthusiastic on-lookers developed, but they were sadly disappointed. Angelina, of course, said "no." In no uncertain terms. Although she did her best to be polite and gentle, she was equally implacable. I was crushed, of course, even though I knew I had no right to be. It was a remarkably stupid idea.

Once again, I begged her to reconsider. I held up the Buccellati diamond, which flashed in the Roman sunlight like a crystal-white flame. I guaranteed her, most insistently, that I *hadn't* changed. In any way. That *nothing* was different. I promised her that everything would be "exactly the same as it was before." I even got angry, saying, "To hell with all those damned Catholic priests and their damned theologies." But nothing worked. It was a total disaster. I was nothing but pathetic, and I knew it, and Angelina knew it, and I didn't care. The bystanders quickly dissipated, finding it too embarrassing to witness such a public humiliation.

Angelina stood up. On the Scalinata. She'd been remarkably calm, even sympathetic. Then she gripped my arm and looked into my eyes with compassion, with sincerity.

"I'm sorry, Bryce, but it's over."

Then she turned away, left the piazza, and I watched her go.

A few days later, on a flight to Milan to cover a story for the *Herald*, I found myself crying uncontrollably. It was rather disgusting and extremely embarrassing, but I was unable to do anything about it.

The flight attendant was very kind and attentive at first, but then she decided that it was best to leave me alone. The other passengers looked away, pretending not to see.

I was helpless.

Nothing like that had ever happened to me before. Never. Neither had depressions, rages, and insomnias. For a long time, I vomited regularly, several times a week, and for months I had chronic headaches. I was so tense at work that I got into regular arguments with my best friend, Eddie Watts, and once I actually started a physical fight, knocking Eddie to the ground. Before it was broken up, there were numerous cuts, numerous minor bruises, and I apologized the very next morning, and several subsequent times. But things between us were never the same, and I was continually ashamed of myself. I couldn't even remember what I was fighting about, and I certainly couldn't fathom my own behavior. I hadn't had a fight since I was a child.

It was crude and demeaning.

Everything seemed demeaning. Every single moment of my useless life without Angelina was degrading and painful.

Assiduously, I tried not to blame anyone else, or anything else, except, of course, myself. But I soon realized that, almost impulsively, I couldn't tolerate the sight of a Roman Catholic church, or a nun, or a priest. On one occasion, I found myself inexplicably raging against Jesus Christ himself. After all, who *is* this long-dead Jew? Who *is* this dead itinerant preacher from the nowheresville deserts of Palestine who'd once had the temerity to say, "He that believeth not, shall be condemned." Or "Heaven and earth shall pass away, but my words shall not pass away." And all the rest of it. Why, after two thousand years, is he still intruding into people's personal lives, making impossible demands, stirring up all kinds of trouble? Plato didn't do that. Neither did Aristotle. Why should Jesus Christ?

About four weeks after the break-up, a package arrived from Fatima. Without thinking, I opened it immediately, tearing away the brown-paper wrapping, staring down at the Hofmann picture. The enigmatic face of Jesus Christ that had been hanging over my uncle's deathbed. *This* was his legacy! *This* was what he'd left behind for his pathetic nephew!

Enraged, I stared into the unfathomable eyes of Hofmann's Christ. Then I lifted up the portrait and smashed it down to the wooden floor of my apartment. The glass shattered all over the place, and the frame smashed apart, but the picture itself was completely unharmed. Which was even more infuriating. Fed-up, I grabbed the picture and angrily shoved it into an unused bureau drawer. Out of sight, out of mind. Later, cleaning up the mess, I cut myself rather badly on a piece of broken glass. Warm red blood dripped down to the hardwood floor.

I was hopeless, desperate, and I knew it. I was suffocating. I felt like a man confined in a tiny dark cell, devoid of his senses, cut off from everyone and everything, trapped within the black chaotic torments of his own disordered mind. It was, I imagined, like drowning, eerily engulfed in a frigid black liquid, sinking downward, flailing uselessly, unable to breathe, grasping for what's not really there.

When I was a boy, the nuns had taught me that despair was the complete and voluntary abandonment of all hope of salvation. But I'd already done that a long time ago, and it had had no discernible effect on my life. Who cares about fantastical unlikely hereafters when all there *really* is is the active present? Be it good. Be it bad. So I knew better. The nuns were wrong. Despair was not not-having some fantasy about life-after-death. Despair was not-having what you needed in *this* life.

Despair was not-having Angelina.

Ernest Dowson, the sad-sack decadent poet of the 1890's, whom I'd read and admired in my lit class at NYU, knew exactly what despair was:

> *And health and hope have gone the way of love,*
> *Into the drear oblivion of lost things.*

Too bad it wasn't a *true* oblivion.

Which would have made things a whole lot easier. But even in my worst moments, even at my most self-destructive, I never felt suicidal. Not on religious grounds, but rather because I somehow harbored the absurdist notion, even *de profundus*, that everything would somehow, in some inexplicable way, manage to rectify itself. That my present debilitation was just a trial of some kind. That I'd not only survive, but that I would, in some as yet unfathomable way, win her back.

Even in the lowest depths of my despair, there was always, simultaneously, the absence of *total* despair. Which is why, as the nuns had taught me as a boy, despair, although a most grievous and mortal sin, wasn't actually the worst possible sin. Which was an active hatred of God, which most often related, ironically, to apostasy and heresy.

Somehow I managed to survive.

No matter how dark and out-of-control my life seemed to be, I was still percipient enough to realize that my only hope was work. To preoccupy myself as much as possible. Every single waking moment. So I worked constantly, night and day. Literally. For several months, I moved into my office at the *Herald*, took on more and more editorial duties, and worked incessantly. My boss, Jack Gerston, who'd calmly waited out the initial storm of my depressions and irascibilities, soon became concerned that I was making myself physically sick with overwork. Which we discussed candidly. Which I resisted at first, but eventually relented.

Naturally, from the beginning of my problems, I'd considered moving away from Rome. But where would I go? I definitely didn't want to go back to Maryland. There was nothing for me back there. In reality, I didn't want to go anywhere. I wanted to stay right where I was, in the heart of Rome. For some reason, I felt compelled to live my troublesome life in the same city as Angelina, even though the thought of it crushed me down every single day.

I did, however, agree to go home for my sister's wedding, and I prepared myself for weeks. The family, of course, knew about the break-up with Angelina, but I was determined not to discuss any of my subsequent problems. But as soon as I arrived in Ocean City, they all instantly apprehended the extent of the damage, although they never pressed me about it. My mother was the only one who actually broached the subject, when we were alone one time, saying simply, "Just be patient, Bryce, it'll pass. It always does." Later, she added, "Remember we're praying for you." Which didn't give me the slightest bit of solace, beyond the obvious fact that I appreciated her love and concern.

The wedding was fine. I served as one of Richard's grooms, and I did the best I could. Later, during the reception, I slipped away and drove to the north end of the Island just off Coastal Highway and parked across the street from the little home where Kimberly and her husband and their young daughter lived. As the twilight began to creep in from the coast, a gray SUV pulled into the driveway, and I watched carefully as Kim, who looked remarkably beautiful, and her lovely little daughter, maybe three years old, walked hand-in-hand into the house. They seemed perfectly happy. They seemed *more* than just happy, and I was glad for Kim. I was glad for them all. Even the husband.

Later that night, long after Ronnie and Richard had flown to the Caribbean, I slipped out of my parents' house and went down to the beach. *My* beach. The winds were sharp and gusty. The sea was black and turbulent. The clouds were low and dark, concealing the hidden moon. It was exactly like the night when Kim had ended everything eight years ago. I walked north, past Blackstone Jetty, to the precise spot where everything had happened.

"Why?" I'd asked her that night eight long years ago.

"Because what's important to me is no longer important to you."

It was that simple, and she was right.

"Maybe it never was," she added, not with reproach, but with sadness and regret.

That fall, I'd come home for Thanksgiving, near the end of my third semester at NYU, and I discovered that the impossible had happened. I'd lost my girlfriend. The only girlfriend I'd ever had, or ever wanted. I'd lost her because I'd gotten slack about attending Mass on Sundays. Because I didn't bother that much about all that Catholic stuff anymore. Because I'd become lukewarm.

Which meant, from Kimberly's point-of-view, that things could never work out as we'd planned. It was impossible, and she'd made up her mind. She was implacable. She sat on the beach in her orange windbreaker, and she cried uncontrollably in the winds and the darkness. Eventually, I sat down beside her, put my arm around her, and felt a terrible desolation in my heart. Not because things were ending, because I really didn't believe that it was possible, surely these problems would blow over in time, but because she was so lovely, so sad.

"We'll work things out, Kim," I said.

But she shook her head, knowing the full truth, crying even more.

So the "one" had gotten rid of me because I was slack, and the "other" had gotten rid of me because she suspected, incorrectly, without a shred of evidence, that I'd somehow rekindled some kind of metaphysical craving.

What a colossal fool I was in Rome.

What a colossal fool I'd been back then in Maryland, when I assumed, rather smugly, that it was just some kind of "good girl thing" that Kimberly was going through. Maybe exacerbated by whatever fears she might have had about whatever I was doing in New York City. But I was wrong, dead wrong, and when I finally realized it, when I finally had to face the fact that I'd been cut out of her life, I was devastated. My whole life seemed worthless and empty. Which it was. I was traumatized for about a year, and I never really got over it until that extraordinary moment when I first looked into Angelina's eyes on that sunny day in Rome.

I sat down on the hard damp Maryland sand, exactly where we'd sat eight years ago, and I thought about how much I loved Kimberly back then, when we were both young and foolish, with a kind of inexhaustible dimensionless love. I pushed it from my mind. I hoped she was happy tonight, and every night, with her pretty little daughter and the husband I'd never met.

Then I thought about my youth in Maryland. It was a marvelous life of contentment, which my wonderful parents had created for me and my younger sister. A world of love, of supportive parents, of spirituality, of easy grades, of fun, of excitement, of friends, of all-star baseball games, of the magnificent ocean, of the magnificent moon, of wonderful Kimberly. It was like a dream that I'd once had. Which I certainly didn't deserve.

Then the disinterested coastal wind blasted a piercing gust down the edge of the beach stinging the surface of my eyes. At the same moment, the whirling clouds parted above me, and the silvery moon briefly emerged, flooding her gleaming lights over the vast expanse of the violent death-black Atlantic. It was awesome, it was awe-inspiring, it was even a bit terrifying, yet somehow comforting. Yes, I thought to myself, I'd once let Kimberly get away, but I wasn't willing to lose Angelina as well. Not forever. So I decided to try one more time. Maybe I'd suffered enough by now. Maybe she'd finally see that I really hadn't changed. Maybe, at last, she'd fully apprehend the stupendous and permanent power of my love.

Two weeks later, fourteen months after the disasters at Trevi Fountain and Scalinata, I waited, surreptitiously, up the street from Parenzo's. When she emerged from the boutique at the end of the day, I followed her to Palazzo Colonna. I was remarkably calm. There'd definitely be no "scene" today. No humiliations. I would do everything possible to make her feel comfortable. But I was determined to find out. To find out if there was any possible chance of reconciliation.

Even the remotest possibility.

Casually, I intercepted Angelina on Via della Pilotta, beneath the bridges, between the palace and Colonna gardens. She was surprised to see me, but not displeased. She was dressed in pinks today, and there was a soft pink ribbon in her hair. As always, she was a vision of impeccable loveliness.

We spoke rather easily, comfortably, not without intimacy.

"How *is* everything, Bryce?" she eventually asked, with interest, with real concern.

"Fine," I said with conviction, "everything's back in order."

Even though it wasn't true.

"I'm sorry," I continued, "that I made you feel so uncomfortable at the Trevi and later at Scalinata. I didn't know what I was doing, and I was afraid of losing you."

"I understand, Bryce, it was difficult for me too. Very difficult."

Oddly, I suddenly realized for the first time that I'd never given that possibility the slightest consideration. I'd never even bothered to consider what Angelina had been going through.

"And you?" I asked. "Is everything OK?"

"Everything's fine, Bryce. Have you heard my good news?"

"No."

"I've been engaged for the past two months," she said rather happily, as if she really believed that I was over her, as if she truly believed that I'd be delighted by her "good news."

I didn't even look down at the diamond that was probably glistening on her left hand because everything went blank. Instantly. Later, I seemed to remember saying "congratulations," and wishing her, with as much enthusiasm as I could muster, "the very best." Then, somehow, I managed to politely extricate myself, as I wandered around the Forum, hour after hour, as if fourteen months hadn't already passed me by, as if I was right back at Trevi Fountain.

Within my embittered heart, I cursed every single thing in my entire life, except her. Especially myself. Especially my damned meddling uncle who'd so arrogantly messed around in my life and managed to destroy it. So much for the great prophet! So much for his message from the grave!

Be worthy and Angelina will be your wife.

Obviously not.

Not by a long shot.

Angelina was about to become someone else's wife, and it was all over. Finished. It seemed to me that the old priest, with his clever deathbed deceits, had proven to be nothing more than a total fraud. Just like the entire, vast, conspiratorial church that he so appropriately represented. The whole damned Catholic sham.

No one knew it better than me.

After all, about a month ago, Vincente Barcelos had been elected pope.

At this very moment, over at the Vatican, a blasphemer, a whore-monger, and an audacious heretic, was sitting on the throne of St. Peter's, brazenly calling himself Pope Peter II.

The Barcelos story, with its quirky alterations of fortune, had been nothing short of remarkable, and I'd followed it closely, with a mixture of disgust and condescension, from my office at the *Herald*. Last April, after eight months in the "wilderness" serving as a chaplain at a small hospital in the Portuguese Algarve, the disgraced Portuguese cardinal had been suddenly and dramatically rehabilitated. The young girl who'd accused him of sexual seduction had appeared at a wild press conference in Lisbon, admitting that she'd fabricated the entire story. Supposedly, she was motivated by her mother's animosity towards the church and her own bitterness about her sister's botched abortion. With her mother's collusion, she'd concocted the entire story about a man she'd never even met.

She seemed perfectly sincere. Her name was Luisa Mendes, she was now sixteen years old, and she'd fallen in love with a young Catholic fisherman from Queluz who wanted to marry her. She claimed that she wanted to reconcile herself with the church and set her life in order. She apologized to pretty much everyone, including every single Catholic in Portugal, and she begged for the cardinal's forgiveness. When the press descended on the Algarve, the cardinal was oddly serene. He had nothing much to say, except to thank God for his good fortune. For the truth. He seemed far more concerned about the well-being of the young girl than about the extraordinary nature of his sudden rehabilitation. His conduct was perfectly exemplary, and no one, not even the anti-papist press in Lisbon, doubted his unqualified innocence.

When they pressed the cardinal, over and over again, about why he'd never bothered to defend himself, and why, over the past year and a half, he'd never even addressed the charges, let alone deny them, he answered, simply:

"I believed I was supposed to be silent. To place my trust in God."

"But if you were innocent," the incredulous reporters called out, "then why didn't you say so?"

"I believed I was supposed to wait and be patient," Barcelos responded, again and again, with obvious sincerity.

"But isn't it wrong," the reporters would ask, "to let a lie go unchallenged? Especially a lie that gives scandal to the church?"

"All I can say," the cardinal repeated, "is that I felt that it was best to place my complete trust in Jesus Christ."

That was the end of it.

Everyone believed the man, even me. Almost immediately, he was reinstated in Lisbon, finding himself even more popular than before. When Pope Marcellus, who'd sent me to Portugal to visit my dying uncle, finally succumbed to cancer, Barcelos, always a curia favorite, was selected as his successor on the first ballot.

What a marvelous story!

What an outrageous sham!

The sinister author of those three heretical books was now the Vicar of Christ on earth, sitting on St. Peter's throne. If the man possessed even the slightest bit of integrity, he would have exposed his authorship of *The Cyrene* and the other two books, recanted his heresies, asked for forgiveness, and stayed at the little hospital in the Algarve. After all, this was a man who'd embezzled from the Church, who'd impregnated a young parishioner, who'd driven her to suicide, who'd wallowed in prostitutes, who'd engaged in satanic rituals, and who'd, at one time, seriously considered homicide. Now he was the beloved, seemingly saintly leader of the largest spiritual communion on the face of earth.

The entire fraudulent Roman Catholic Church.

A number of times, I seriously considered exposing the man myself. As a reporter, I knew the available evidence was extremely weak, but I also felt reasonably certain that I could track down his beach house, and quite a bit more, after a few days of serious snooping around in Portugal. Nevertheless, despite my outrage, despite my disgust, I decided not to bother. Why should I care? Yes, the whole thing was revolting, but it was also, in a way, perfectly appropriate. A sham pope for a sham church. Why not? Besides, I really didn't want to get involved again. For well over a year, I'd been trying, with varying success, to forget about my ill-fated trip to Fatima and its ugly ramifications in my personal life.

So I forgot about it, and I continued on, exactly as before: hyper-busy at work, always alone, perpetually discontent. The next ten months passed by quickly, each one a void, each one a blank. Eventually, word of Angelina's wedding, of her "happiness," of her honeymoon in Rio, came and went. I got drunk for two full days, something I'd never done before in my entire life, then immediately went back to work, to my existential blankness.

Finally, on one particularly hectic day, which seemed like all the rest of my days, I was covering a story in the Testaccio section of Rome, where I seldom went, and I was walking down a side street off Via Marmorata, and I passed a little chapel named for San Gerardo. As usual, I found myself instinctively repelled by the sight of the little Catholic church, and everything it stood for, but I had to admit, I was irresistibly intrigued by this sudden and unanticipated conjuring of "St. Gerard."

Whom my uncle had mentioned in his message to Barcelos.

I stopped abruptly in the middle of the street and stared at the old stone chapel. Despite making a futile effort to resist, I couldn't contain my curiosity. Without any further thought, I ascended the chapel steps and entered inside. It was cool, empty, and dark. I passed through a small vestibule, and, inexplicably, took a seat in one of the back pews for a moment. Resting. Today, like every other day, I was much more tired than I was willing to admit. Casually, I glanced up at the distant crucifix over the main altar. It was a bloody and graphic Christ, so I looked away.

Not seeing a priest anywhere, I decided to go back to the vestibule and look around for some information about St. Gerard. It didn't take long. There was a stack of little pamphlets which sketched the history of the church, built by the Italian monarchy back in 1878, which also contained a brief summary of the life of St. Gerard, who was, apparently, the patron saint of expectant mothers.

I took one of the pamphlets, returned to my seat in the chapel, and read about the life of the saint.

Gerard Majella was born in Muro Lucano in Neapolitan Italy in 1726. After serving as a tailor's apprentice and a much-abused manservant, he entered the Redemptorists as a lay brother in 1749. His sanctity was so remarkable, so renowned, that it merited the praise of the great Alphonsus Liguori. He was also well-known for extraordinary ecstasies, miraculous healings, bilocations, prophecies (including the date of his own death), and the ability to read the thoughts of the countless people who came to him for religious counsel, even though he wasn't actually a priest.

Then, from seemingly nowhere, a pregnant young woman stepped forward and accused him of fathering her unborn child. Oddly enough, Majella retreated into silence and refused to respond to the charges. As a result, he was isolated by his baffled superiors, who put him under surveillance and cut him off from the sacraments. Eventually, several months later, the young woman admitted that she'd fabricated the entire story. No one doubted the truth of her recantation, and when the Redemptorists asked their greatly maligned brother why he'd never bothered to defend himself, he said, rather innocently, that he thought that's how one was supposed to behave in the face of an unjust accusation. In the aftermath, Gerard's clearly sanctified life continued exactly as before, until he died in 1755 at the young age of twenty-nine, on the exact day he'd predicted, at the Redemptorist house in Caposele, where he'd humbly served as porter.

I was stunned.

I immediately recalled that terribly depressing day in Lisbon two years ago and my subsequent and most peculiar night at Cabo da Roca.

I remembered, word for word, the brief message that my uncle had left for his close friend Vincente Cardinal Barcelos:

Before Rome, St. Gerard.

Which happened.

Which happened *exactly*.

On the day following my uncle's death, the cardinal had been accused of a sexual crime, responded with silence like St. Gerard, and, eventually, was exonerated and elected pope!

As the little pamphlet pointed out, St. Gerard was not only the patron of expectant mothers, he was also the patron of the "falsely accused."

It was too fantastic to be a coincidence. My uncle, like the pious doorkeeper from the kingdom of Naples, must have had inexplicable prophetic powers, just as Barcelos had claimed in Lisbon. But what about *my* message? Was it still possible? Was there still hope for an eventual reconciliation with Angelina? Despite the fact that she was now, apparently, a happily married woman?

I remembered what Barcelos told me that day in Lisbon, half-drunk, completely demoralized, when I asked him about the young girl and her charges:

I never touched that girl. I don't even know who she is. It's a penance, don't you understand that?

Well, maybe *now* I understood it.

It *really* had been a "penance." Barcelos had borne it nobly, been subsequently rehabilitated, and the prophecy had come true. Maybe all of my own sufferings over the past two years had been a similar kind of penance, even though I never fully realized it, and maybe, as a result, my own prophecy would also come to pass. It was a wildly exhilarating possibility, but I was naturally wary of more false hopes in my life, so I pushed it from my mind.

Temporarily.

But what about Barcelos?

So what if he'd done his year and a half of penance? The man was still a heretic, still a blasphemer, still the perpetrator of all kinds of reprehensible behavior. How could he possibly become the pope? The church teaches that it's possible for even the most stupendous sinners to be forgiven their mistakes, but this seemed way too much. Why should the man be rewarded with the papacy itself? Why not let him live out his life in the Portuguese Algarve? Why should Barcelos, of all the cardinals in the world, become the Bishop of Rome? It was absurd. It was unjust.

Why had my uncle wished it to be so?

It made no sense, and the more I searched for answers, the more I conjured up even more unanswerable questions. Of all kinds. As I sat there for three long interminable hours, all alone in the back of the chapel. Finally, I was forced to accept the fact that my curiosity was back. Like that stormy night on Cabo da Roca, I felt an inordinate irresistible craving to "know." To comprehend. To understand. I had no interest in "chasing after God," and I certainly hadn't planned to chase after him in Cabo da Roca. All I wanted was the truth. All I wanted was to apprehend the truth about the ridiculous life that I was living, and living so badly.

Why not?

I stood up and left the chapel, without ever glancing back at the crucifix and its tortured Christ. Then I walked to the nearest bookstore and purchased the English version of *Rennes-le-Château: The Mystery of Christ*. This was where I needed to start. To try and fathom the mind of the man who'd somehow become the Catholic pope.

Finding an outdoor café near Parco Testaccio, I sat down at an isolated table and read the entire book with total absorption.

With unsettling fascination.

In the first paragraph of the first chapter, the alleged author, "Bernardi Sorel," explained that "the greatest mystery in human history," meaning "the mystery of Jesus Christ," was best apprehended in the modern era by first examining the mystery of Béranger Saunière, an obscure village curé who'd became fabulously wealthy in 1891.

Béranger Saunière: Born in 1852, Saunière was a handsome charming Catholic priest who in 1885 was assigned to the tiny, rural, hilltop parish of Rennes-le-Château in southern France, not far from Carcassonne, not far from the Pyrenees. Six years later, while attempting to restore the church's main altar, he discovered four Parchment documents inside one of the Visigothic pillars that supported the altar slab.

The Documents: Two of the parchments were genealogies of local families. The other two were New Testament texts that were obviously encoded. The most easily decipherable message was:

To Dagobert II, king, and to Sion belongs this treasure, and it is death.

The latter few words, it seems, could also be transcribed as: "he is dead there." Dagobert II was a Seventh Century French king, the last of the Merovingians. Saunière was able to ascertain that the documents had been sealed in the pillar around the time of the French Revolution by a previous curé at Rennes-le-Château, the Abbé Antoine Bigou. Unable to make further progress with the parchments, Saunière went to the Bishop of Carcassonne, who sent him to Paris.

Paris: In Paris, while consulting with Abbé Bieil, the director of St. Sulpice and an expert in cryptography, Saunière became friends with the Abbé's brilliant nephew, Emile Hoffet, who had numerous occultist associates in Paris, even though he was studying to become a priest. As a result, the charismatic country priest suddenly found himself swept into an elite Parisian circle of artists and intellectuals that included Mallarmé, Maeterlinck, Debussy, and the famous soprano, Emma Calvé, with whom Saunière initiated a sexual liaison. Eventually, before leaving Paris, Saunière visited the Louvre where he purchased three reproductions including one by Nicolas Poussin.

Et in Arcadia Ego: The Poussin's picture, which obviously had great personal significance for the artist since he insisted that it be engraved on his tomb, depicts three shepherds studying an isolated tombstone in the countryside. A woman stands close by, and one of the shepherds, gesturing to the young woman, points to the inscription on the stone, "*Et in Arcadia Ego*," meaning, "I [death] am also present in Arcadia." The Latin text of the quote is also an anagram for "*I tego arcana Dei*," meaning, "Begone, I conceal the secrets of God."

The Return to Rennes-le-Château: Returning to his mountain parish, Saunière immediately dug up the stone slab set in the floor before the altar, finding a carving on its underside (which depicted mounted knights) and two skeletons. He then sealed up his church, and with Marie Denarnaud, his housekeeper and lover, he began wandering around the countryside, then lugging sacks of unknown content back to the church, informing the curious that he was simply collecting stones for a grotto in his garden. During one of these expeditions, which invariably took place near various graveyards, Saunière removed the headstone of a local noblewoman who'd died in 1781. He also defaced the inscriptions on the stone slab that covered her grave.

The Grave of Marie, Marquise de Blanchefort: The wealthy Blanchefort family, which had ancient Cathar associations, had once included Bertrand de Blanchefort, the Fourth Grand Master of the Knights Templar. The defaced inscriptions on the Marquise's stone slab (which were recorded by a local antiquary) were "*Et in Arcadia Ego*" and "*Réddis Régis Cellis Arcis*," meaning, "At Royal Reddis [an ancient name for Rennes-le-Château] in the cave of the fortress." The inscriptions also contained two rather obvious code words, or key-words: *Mort* and *Epée*, which would eventually prove crucial in deciphering the coded parchments. Significantly, the Marquise's headstone had been designed by Abbé Antoine Bigou, the same priest who'd originally concealed the four parchments in the altar pillar.

The Treasure: The fact that the less-than-pious rural priest Béranger Saunière suddenly became inexplicably wealthy is a matter of historical record. Not long after his return from Paris, he began spending prodigious sums of money. He built a new road to his hilltop location, along with a brand-new water supply. He built a luxurious villa for himself, with a tropical garden and elaborate fountains. He also constructed a rather peculiar gothic tower, almost like an observation post, to house his ever-expanding library. Given his marked predilection for material possessions, he began purchasing rare Chinas, valuable antiques, and expensive fabrics. He ate only the finest imported foods and wines, and he began to entertain lavishly, even hosting such distinguished guests as the Archduke Johann von Habsburg, who was the cousin of Franz-Josef, the current Emperor of Austria. He also undertook a complete restoration of the church, including many curious and bizarre details like the inscription over the door, "*Terribilis Est Locus Iste*," meaning "This place is terrible," and a sinister statue of the demon Asmodeus, the reputed guardian of Solomon's treasure.

Inquiries: When the Bishop of Carcassonne asked the parish priest about his new-found wealth, Saunière informed him, rather boldly, that he was unable to divulge the source, and the bishop decided not to press him any further. The subsequent Bishop of Carcassonne was not so tolerant. When Saunière refused to answer his questions, he was suspended from his position. Eventually, there were three official inquiries into Saunière's activities, and three sentences were passed, all of which the serenely confident curé completely ignored. Finally, the fed-up bishop ordered the transfer of the rebellious priest, but Saunière absolutely refused to leave. Even when the new priest, Abbé Marty, arrived in Rennes-le-Château, Saunière remained right where he was in his opulent villa, while the new priest was forced to reside in dilapidated living quarters within the church. In 1915, Fr. Béranger Saunière was officially defrocked, but he didn't seem to mind at all.

Death: Two years later, in January 1917, the ex-priest died in his villa, apparently from cirrhosis of the liver. He was sixty-four years of age, and he'd lived in Rennes-le-Château for the past thirty-two years. On his deathbed, he was visited by a local priest, Abbé Riviére, who was so horrified by what the defrocked priest told him that he refused to give Saunière the last rites. According to the historian Gérard de Sède, Fr. Riviére was severely traumatized by the experience, falling into depressions, becoming a recluse, and, supposedly, "never smiling again."

Marie Denarnaud: Saunière's longtime lover and collaborator was his only heir. She maintained herself in luxury, often wearing expensive jewelry and clothes, until her death in 1956. She remained loyally devoted to Saunière and never revealed the secret of his wealth, but she did remark, on various occasions, that "The people of Rennes-le-Château are walking on gold, and they don't even know it." Nearing her death, she decided to sell the villa to Noel Corbu, whom she promised to tell a secret that would make him both rich and powerful. She then suffered a stroke and was rendered speechless on her deathbed.

Gérard de Sède: The first book published about the strange story of Béranger Saunière and the treasure of Rennes-le-Château was a popular account written by Albert Salamon which appeared in France in 1956. But the most intriguing book relating to the unsolved mystery was Gérard de Sède's fascinating *Le Trésor Maudit* (*The Accursed Treasure*) which was first published in 1967. Among other things, de Sède claimed to have deciphered a crucial message in the longer of the two Biblical parchments found in the altar's pillar. He did so, he claimed, by using the keywords *mort* and *epée*, along with an extremely complicated cryptographic process known as the Vigenère Method.

The Encoded Message:

Shepherdess without temptation to which Poussin and Teniers hold the key Peace 681 with the cross and the Horse of God I reach this Demon Guardian at midday blue apples.

This oddly convoluted text (still mostly unexplicated) is believed by most Rennes-le-Château historians to have led Saunière to his treasure, although *how* he could have possibly decrypted the text is still uncertain and debatable. But the text clearly directs attention back to the Poussin picture, *Et in Arcadia Ego*, which de Sède associates in his book with the mysterious Priory, a secret and powerful underground brotherhood of elitist conspirators.

The Priory of Sion: The most "secret of all secret societies," whose grandmasters supposedly included Nicolas Flamel, da Vinci, Newton, Hugo, and Debussy (whom Saunière had met in Paris), was allegedly associated with the Knights Templar and even, later, the Rosicrucians and the Masons. It was fanatically dedicated to restoring, in any way possible, the Merovingian bloodline to the throne of France. The Merovingian Dynasty, founded by King Clovis at the commencement of the Sixth Century, died out with the assassination of King Dagobert II in 679. Dagobert, who had a lance driven through his eye while he was asleep, was murdered by associates of the forthcoming dynasty that would rise up and eventually replace the Merovingians: the Carolingians, whose first king was Pepin the Short.

So what did all these historical curiosities have to do with the "mystery of Christ" which Sorel promised to reveal in the contents of his book? So far, it wasn't clear, but the author told his story with such fascinating detail, such breathless pace, such authoritative yet unobtrusive scholarship, that I remained perfectly patient, even satisfied, as I continued reading. I was *more* than willing to wait, and I imagined that every other reader of the book must have felt the same way. Then, without pausing for a moment, I proceeded into the middle section of the book which examined the plethora of possible solutions to *what* the treasure was. And *where* it might have come from.

The Treasure of the Visigoths: After the Visigoths had plundered Rome in 410, they eventually brought their enormous wealth to southern France where they set up a Visigoth empire with Toulouse as their capital. Eventually, after a relentless attack by Clovis and the Franks, they moved their treasure to Carcassonne near Rennes-le-Château. Years later, Dagobert himself had been married to a Visigoth princess. Had Béranger Saunière somehow unearthed the fantastical Roman plunder of the Visigoths?

The Treasure of the Cathars: The great Manichean heresy of the "pure ones" infiltrated into southern France from the Balkans in the Eleventh Century. Believing that the world was created by Satan, they rejected everything physical as totally evil (including all matter, including the world itself, including all human existence, food, sex, etc.). Somehow, they found favor with the excessively tolerant Counts of Toulouse, and they defiantly challenged Rome. Eventually, the northern French nobles and the Papacy combined to initiate a crusade against the Cathars, also known as the Albigensians, in 1209, which was led by Simon de Montfort. It was a brutal campaign, culminating in a ten-month siege of the mountaintop citadel of Montségur. Before the final capitulation of the Cathars, and the subsequent immolation of approximately two hundred heretics who refused to recant, a small group of Albigensians managed to escape with the spectacular "Treasure of the Cathars," taking it, as some claimed, to the nearby town of Rennes-le-Château.

The Treasure of the Templars: It's an indisputable historical fact that the heroic warrior-monks of the Crusades became enormously wealthy. They became the principal bankers of Europe, and their power and wealth eventually proved much too tempting for the unscrupulous king of France, ironically known as Philip the Fair (relating to his handsome appearance). In a stunningly audacious move in 1307, the king arrested every single member of the order in France, and they were summarily tortured. Then, by effectively bullying the pope and orchestrating various other diplomatic machinations, Philip effected the complete termination of the order in 1312. As a result, he was able to appropriate some of the Templars' great wealth, but he was never able to get his greedy hands on their legendary treasure at Bezu, a major Templar stronghold in southern France not far from Rennes-le-Château.

The Treasure of Solomon's Temple: In 70 A.D., Titus sacked Jerusalem and plundered the Third Temple (Herod's Temple), seizing the extraordinary Treasures of Solomon. The historical record shows that Titus brought his booty, including, possibly, the still-existent Ark of the Covenant, back to Rome, as clearly depicted on the Arch of Titus, constructed in 81 A.D. Had the Visigoths found it intact when they'd plundered Rome in 410? If they did, it would have ended up in southern France.

Other Possibilities: As with all such unsolved mysteries, there seems no limit to the endless possibilities, and no limits to the fertile imaginations of those who write speculative books claiming to solve the mystery. To illustrate this fact, "Sorel" briefly listed a catalogue of other reputed sources of Saunière's wealth: that he was paid by the Priory of Sion for unknown services; that he'd discovered the Sangreal (the Holy Grail); that he'd simply robbed various ancient tombs of their contents, using the parchments as his guide; that he'd blackmailed wealthy parishioners with secrets he'd heard in the confessional; that he'd engaged in Black Magic rituals (specifically the sexual Convocation of Venus) with his lovers Marie Denarnaud and Emma Calvé, thus being rewarded by the demon, possibly with the lucrative ability to prophesy for wealthy patrons; that he'd discovered the long-sought-after Philosopher's Stone (or possibly the Elixir of Life); that he'd unearthed the Emerald Tablet of the Egyptian Hermes Trismegistus or possibly the mysterious Urim and Thummim cited in the Old Testament; that he'd discovered an opening into the "Fourth Dimension"; and, finally, inevitably, that he'd somehow made contact with extraterrestrials.

All of these curiosities were summarily dismissed by Sorel in his book, but there was one more fascinating possibility that he wanted to examine in detail: the theory that Saunière had discovered an awesome earth-shattering secret about the life of Jesus Christ, and that he was "paid-off" lavishly to maintain his silence by the Vatican and its wealthy political allies. Thus the third and final section of Sorel's book deftly guides its readers through what the author refers to as "The Magdalene Thesis," which was first proposed by Henry Lincoln, a British Rennes-le-Château investigator. Lincoln's thesis was based on the claims of a lapsed and still-anonymous Anglican clergyman, who asserted that he'd heard the secret from Canon Alfred Leslie Lilley, a man with verifiable connections to St. Sulpice in Paris, and a man who'd definitely known Emile Hoffet, the brilliant young linguist who'd befriended Saunière during his trip to Paris in 1891.

The Secret of all Secrets: That Jesus Christ had *not* died on the cross.

The Plot: Henry Lincoln, following the old "Passover Plot" allegations, suggests that Christ meticulously planned his survival on the cross, allowing himself to be drugged when the sponge was lifted to his lips. Sorel, of course, dismisses this highly improbable and unsupportable conjecture, and suggests instead a Cyrenian solution: that Jesus Christ, the sublime and supremely-magnanimous supra-human creature (although, of course, not quite God) had pre-arranged, with a willing volunteer (the suicidal Simon of Cyrene), to stage a Crucifixion for the necessary edification of all human beings, to teach them how to sacrifice, to teach them how to think of others before themselves, to teach them how to endure their human sufferings with heroic stoicism.

After the Crucifixion of Simon: Having completed the preaching and theological phase of his life, the still-young Jesus Christ left his infant church in Palestine in the capable hands of his co-conspirator, Simon Peter. Then he migrated north, with a few disciples, including his wife, Mary Magdalene. He travelled through Asia Minor, then crossed the Balkans, eventually settling in southern France where he established himself as a temporal power in the region. Mary bore him several sons, and he established a blood dynasty before his unexpected death in 45 A.D. (his tomb being the subject of the Poussin painting). The name of the dynasty, of course, was the Merovingians, and this was the *real* secret of the Priory of Sion (and their supposed allies the Knights Templar) who'd dedicated themselves and their lives to the restoration of the lineage of Jesus Christ to the throne of France. And to other countries as well. The members of the Priory were also, it seems, assiduous agents of the Habsburgs, who traced their roots back to the Merovingians through the House of Lorraine. Thus to Jesus Christ.

I shut the book and sat silently in the twilight, staring into the darkening Parco Testaccio. The little café was busy at the moment, but everyone was preoccupied and discreet. There were still a few empty tables, so I felt no compulsion to hurry myself.

Besides, I was completely overwhelmed. Sorel's third book, just like *The Cyrene*, was an absolute masterpiece of deception. It read like a novel. Even better. It was virtually impossible to put it down. It was clever, cunning, and carefully seductive. Although always careful to praise Jesus Christ, it managed to "dissolve" his divinity with exactly the same praise. Surely such a pernicious book had damaged the faith of thousands of people, if not millions. Who could possibly read it and not wonder? Who could possibly read the book and not come away admiring Christ as a man? Who could possibly read the book and still confidently affirm that Christ was "one with the Father," that he was the "Logos" of St. John, that he was, in fact, divine?

No one.

This was the insidious work of Vincente Barcelos, the current pope of the universal Roman Catholic Church.

It was hard to believe, and I wished, in some inexplicable way, that it wasn't true.

Finally, as I'd done two years ago when I'd read *The Cyrene* in a single sitting at the Biblioteca Nacional in Lisbon, I reopened the book and looked at the preface. It was two short pages of mostly nothing, signed by Bernardi Sorel, located in Lisbon. Then, on impulse, I turned back to the copyright page to look for an imprimatur. Had Barcelos been brazen enough to approve his own book? I guess not. There was no imprimatur anywhere. He'd been far too clever, too cautious, to give himself away.

But there was something else.

The copyright. The original copyright for the text was registered in Lyon. I was stunned. My mind began racing wildly, almost out of control. For the first time, I seemed to apprehend the truth. To apprehend what had always been so perfectly obvious if I hadn't been so foolish and unthinkingly self-absorbed.

Of course!

Everything flooded back into my mind. Everything about those two terrible days in Portugal, which, in effect, had ruined my life: my earlier meeting with Pope Marcellus in the Pinacoteca, the horrors of my uncle's deathbed confession, my eventual departure from Fatima (waving goodbye to little Francisco), my meeting with António Zamora in Lisbon, my bizarre encounter with Barcelos, and my "dark night" on the Atlantic coast at Cabo da Roca.

Through all of it, though all of those unforgettable memories, the little boy's message, for some inexplicable reason, kept ringing in my head. Over and over. It was lovely. It was melodic, like a little song. I could still remember it perfectly, even though I didn't know what it meant.

Impulsively, I took out my phone and called the Portuguese Embassy in Rome. But it was too late in the day. I was put on hold, and I couldn't wait. I turned around to face the various patrons in the café who were eating their evening meals engrossed in their pleasant, private, and discreet conversations.

I called out, loudly, with a bit too much desperation in my voice:

"*C'é qualcuno quà che parla Portoghese?*

When there was no response, I repeated my question in English:

"Does anyone here speak Portuguese?"

It was obvious that everyone in the café recognized both my distress and my good intentions. Despite the abrupt and impolite interruption, they wanted to help, but it seemed that no one spoke the language. Until a pleasant-looking young man gestured with his hand, and I walked over to his table. He was sitting with a pretty young girl who was, like him, in her early twenties.

The young man spoke in an Italian-accented but excellent English.

"My girlfriend's from Oporto," he said quite simply, directing my attention to the young woman sitting beside him.

I nodded at them both, then addressed the girlfriend.

"Can you tell me what this means?"

Even before she had a chance to react, I recited Francisco's message:

"Submeta-se, outro guarda virá."

It presented no problem. The young girl responded immediately, in perfectly clear English:

Submit yourself, another guardian will come.

Chapter 8

St-Tropez

(Wednesday, July 31st)

Heading south for the beaches, my taxi drove quickly through the small Provençal fishing village, with its pretty pastel houses, its picturesque harbor, and its countless luxury yachts bobbing up-and-down in the deep-blue Mediterranean. In the distant past, the tiny fishing port of St-Tropez had attracted Maupassant and Signac and Matisse and Bonnard and Picasso and Colette and Prévert, along with many others, but its international renown was actually based on the sexual insouciance of a young Parisian woman famous for her nakedness, and not much else. Except, maybe, her seductive pout.

However accurate the title of the French film *Et Dieu Créa la Femme* might be, it was the film's director, Roger Vadim, who created Brigitte Bardot in 1956, turning "St-Trop" into the jet-set capital of Côte d'Azur. If not the entire world. Becoming the absolute pinnacle of *français* chic and a haven for all the free-spirited, liberated, well-to-do youth of Europe. Virtually overnight, the little town came to symbolize sexual immorality, high fashion, and wealth, becoming the trendy hot spot, the with-it destination, for the Parisian glitterati. Even the Parisian Existentialists. Soon bohemian elites from all over Europe were descending on the forty, beautiful, sunny beaches southeast of St-Tropez, where countless, liberated, Bardotish young women began swimming and sunbathing topless, occasionally placing Coca Cola bottlecaps over their nipples to stave off the curiosity of the bewildered local gendarmes.

Ironically, the village also had a powerful religious past, being named for the courageous Catholic martyr, St. Torpes, who'd served as a Christian military officer under the Roman Emperor Nero, before being decapitated by imperial command in Pisa in 65 A.D. Afterwards, in a sadistically perverse effort to further denigrate the dead man's reputation, his torso was placed in a small boat with a dog and a cock, who would naturally, it was assumed, devour the corpse after being set to sea. But the little boat drifted northwest to Athenopolis on the southern coast of modern-day France, where the saint's miraculously untouched remains were discovered and preserved. Eventually, centuries later, the little port town took the name of the much revered and martyred saint.

I arrived at the villa late in the afternoon, with the sun still blazing high in the sky. Given my resources at the *Herald*, I had little difficulty tracking the man down.

His isolated beach house was light blue in color, both chic and perfectly appropriate to its location just south of the cape between Plage des Salines and Plage de Tahiti, the latter being the most famous and notoriously decadent beach on the entire Ramatuella Peninsula.

I got out of my taxi, paid the driver, and then, for a few self-collecting moments, I stared at the distant dark mountains, the Massif des Maures. Finally, I walked up to the front door of the beachhouse, passing the shiny-red Alfa Romeo Spider-convertible that was parked in the driveway. When there was no response, I went around to the back of the house and ascended onto a spacious wooden porch that extended over a rather spectacular stretch of the sandy beach and the stunning-blue Mediterranean.

Raxx was sitting, rather idly, in a comfortable lounge chair beneath a large light-blue umbrella. He was facing the ocean, and he seemed to be wearing nothing but a white terrycloth robe. His appearance was perfectly hideous, even disgusting. He looked nothing like the vigorous, not-quite-fiftyish Jesuit that I'd seen at my uncle's bedside. He was now shockingly emaciate, virtually skeletal, and his taut dissipated flesh had been singed to an almost unnatural darkness by the bright Côte d'Azur sun. His face was nothing less than a death's-head, with its overly tanned skin drawn tightly back across the ridges of his skull, giving an unnatural prominence to his moist, dark, bloodshot, and ever-peering eyes.

The heretic looked up.

At me.

"Ah, the nephew," he said, with sarcasm. "I thought you'd pop up eventually."

He spoke with a precise, sophisticated, and cosmopolitan English. His intonations were those of the overly educated, but there was an accompanying aspect of harshness, even hoarseness, that was clearly the result of the man's infirmities. I realized, as I stood in the sunlight, that I'd never actually heard the man's voice before, since he hadn't spoken a word at Fatima.

Here in St-Tropez, the cadaverous man obviously enjoyed hearing himself speak, and he even smiled at his own superciliousness, apparently too weak to actually laugh.

He continued.

"You've come looking for something, haven't you, young man? Snooping around for God-knows-what. You're a reporter, am I correct?"

I nodded.

"Yes, just another apostate reporter," he summed up. "How perfectly ordinary. How perfectly banal."

He positively reeked with condescension, but I was strangely unaffected. Maybe because I was still overwhelmed by the man's revolting and debilitated appearance.

"What is it?" I asked, meaning the illness, which he understood.

"Cancer," he said with a certain bravado. "We've become close companions. I sit here much of the day staring out at the sea, thinking about all kinds of things, as the cancer silently metastasizes within me with a reckless abandon. It's rather odd to be fully conscious that your own physical-self is gleefully self-destructing."

He nearly laughed.

He tried and failed.

"When did you find out?"

"The day after your uncle died. It was just a routine test, but the results were a bit of a bombshell."

He stared at me intensely.

"I guess we *really* are punished for our sins," he said with a smirk.

"Do you believe that?" I wondered, expecting more sarcasm.

"Maybe I do," the heretic said, evasively, dismissively.

"Why am I here?" I asked, assuming that Raxx might know.

"Just to pester me, I suppose, to be a nuisance," the one-time Jesuit responded, a bit impatiently. "I suppose you'd like me to tell you that God exists, that God is good, that Christ is God. Well, the answers are 'maybe,' 'not especially,' and 'who cares?'"

I didn't know how to respond, so I looked out towards the beach and noticed, for the first time, that a young woman was sunbathing not far away.

"My whore," he explained. "It might surprise you, given my condition, that I can still indulge my multifarious pleasures. Good food, good books, the sun, her considerable sexual skills, and more and more, of course, the drugs. I'm flush with morphine right now, and I'm feeling just fine."

Unconvinced, I turned back and looked at the man.

He pointed at a little table right next to his chair.

"These are my favorites."

I looked down at the table. There was a small crystal dish with a number of slightly stained sugar cubes. Beside the dish, there was a small prescription bottle, a glass of water, and a handgun. It was a blued semi-automatic of some kind, maybe a Beretta.

"Acid?" I said, referring to the sugar cubes.

"Yes, I'll be dropping another one a little bit later, right after the sun goes down. I look forward to it. Quite a bit. After all, I don't have much time left, and I fully intend to make the best of it."

"You don't look like you have *any* time left," I said.

He didn't bother to conceal his irritation.

"What are you supposed to be, anyway?" he asked rhetorically. "The harbinger of death?"

Once again, I didn't respond.

"Well, maybe you are," he said and smiled. "Just like the half-wit little curé who showed up yesterday afternoon talking gibberish about the last sacrament. He was quite pathetic and irritatingly insistent. When I couldn't get him to leave me alone, I told my slut to strip off her clothes, which she did, and he left immediately."

Raxx's memory of the fleeing priest incited something close to a laugh, but I wasn't about to be diverted.

"I think you could die any minute," I insisted, not knowing why I felt that way, except for the man's ghoulish appearance.

Once again, Raxx looked at me fixedly. He seemed almost serpentine. He also seemed fully cognizant of the fact that he *really* did look rather serpentine, but he didn't seem to mind at all.

"Don't worry, jackass," he responded, "I'm not dying today. You know why?"

I shook my head.

"Because it's the feast of Ignatius Loyola, and surely the good-god-in-heaven wouldn't want me messing with that little celebration, would he?"

When I said nothing, the heretic continued to eye me intensely, suspiciously.

"Why are you here?" he asked bluntly.

"I don't know."

He wasn't convinced, but he didn't press it any further.

I continued.

"Do you really believe all the garbage you wrote in your Sorel books?"

He seemed totally unconcerned that I knew that he was the true author of the heretical Sorel books.

"Some of it," he answered, enjoying his coyness.

"What about Rennes-le-Château?"

"Wouldn't you like to know?" he replied with another smirk.

Then he leaned over toward his Beretta, picked up a little bronze bell, and shook it twice.

Immediately, the young woman on the beach rose from her blanket. She wore large shades, and she was topless. Quickly, she gathered up her things and came to the back porch. She paid absolutely no attention to me, as if she'd been instructed not to acknowledge any of Raxx's visitors, and she looked down at the emaciate man in the lounge chair, ready to please him in any way possible. She was somewhere in her mid-twenties, quite voluptuous, quite attractive, and completely devoid of shame.

"Vichyssoise," he commanded.

Then he looked over at me.

"Would my guest like some soup?"

I shook my head.

The thought of food made me nauseous.

"Maybe you'd rather have *her* instead?" Raxx suggested. "She'll be more than willing. I pay her well."

The young woman was completely unconcerned, totally subservient. Her humiliation was so complete that it was no longer conscious.

I shook my head, and Raxx nodded at the young woman, who entered the back of the beachhouse. When she was gone, the dying man smiled with pleasure at my obvious discomfort.

"Uneasy?"

I shrugged.

"Well, *everything* in this life is uneasy, young man. That's the way it is. That's the way god made it, abetted by men like your uncle. They're never content unless they make you feel uneasy, or inadequate, or guilty about something."

"That's not true," I said, not really thinking much about what I was saying. Just trying, inadequately, to defend my dead uncle.

"But it *is* true," he assured me. "It's why you ducked the old bastard for over five years. Or was it seven? Ever since the day you discovered that a little apostasy made your frivolous life a whole lot easier."

I didn't dispute it.

"As for me, I'm perfectly willing to detest the both of them," he admitted, meaning both God and my uncle. "Along with Ignatius, Aquinas, our pathetic new pope, and all the countless silly scholars who willfully submit their intellectual imaginations to metaphysical rubbish. Not to mention the millions of totally pathetic people who live out their shallow lives in fear and submission, especially, most especially, all those stupid, damned, apostate reporters like yourself. In fact, I detest almost everything. I even detest, to be perfectly thorough, the demon himself."

For a moment, Raxx allowed his animus to mitigate.

Then he continued.

"Yes, that's correct, I tried out the Light-bearer for a while, just as your uncle revealed at Fatima. I tried his rituals, his oaths, and his boorish perversities, both at Lyon and Rennes, but nothing much came of it. Either before your uncle's death or afterwards. I was offered nothing in return. No insight, no power, no miraculous cancer cure!"

He laughed at the idea.

"I suppose Lucifer felt confident that he *had* me already."

He was amused, and I was stunned by his indifference.

"Have you no repentance at all?"

"None."

He spoke with defiance, anger.

"Do you know the motto of Satan?"

"No," I admitted.

He scoffed.

"You don't seem to know much of anything, do you, young man?"

When I made no attempt to defend myself, Raxx continued.

"*Non serviam*. That's what Satan announced to God, 'I Will Not Serve,' and I agree with him entirely, although I refuse to serve either one of them. Not the Light-bearer. Not his supposedly divine tormentor."

Since I had no response, I shifted the subject.

"What was your message?"

"What was yours?"

I told him.

"Be worthy and Angelina will be your wife."

"So where's Miss Angelina right now?"

"Married to someone else."

"Yeah, in someone else's bed. Never trust a prophet, young man! They're even more unreliable than the heretics."

He seemed quite pleased with himself.

"But let's face it," he continued, "prophets are rather fascinating, right? I bet you've still got your little message hidden away somewhere. I bet you can't quite throw it away, right? Even though you know it's rubbish."

He was right, of course, and he *knew* he was right.

"Well," he added, "don't feel too humiliated about it. I've still got mine too. It's on my bedroom wall. You can check it out before you leave."

He paused.

"That's assuming, of course, that I *let* you leave."

Which was clearly a threat of some kind.

Suddenly, he squirmed in his chair, uncomfortably. The pain was back. Immediately, he leaned over and picked up his little prescription bottle and the glass of water.

"Excuse me, the morph's wearing off, and I find pain a most unpleasant and distracting sensation."

He swallowed a little red pill, having some trouble getting it down his throat.

"What's the gun for?" I asked.

"What are *all* guns for," he said, as if it was a stupid question. Then he stared at me with an odd mixture of intimidation and playfulness.

"Maybe *that's* why you came," he suggested rather ominously.

Then, once again, the cancer-pain surged up from somewhere within him, and the heretic winced. When he recovered, he seemed angry.

"I know why you're here," he said with irritation. "You've come to 'save' me."

I was stunned by the idea.

It was preposterous.

"I realize that you're too stupid to know what you're doing, but that's the *real* reason that you're here, as ridiculous as it seems. Yes, the silly, little, know-nothing newspaper hack, with no faith in God or anything else, has traveled all the way to the beaches of St-Tropez to save the great heretic. You know why? Because somewhere in the hidden recesses of your pathetic little mind, you can't stand to see me die so content, so unrepentant, so unsubmissive to something that neither one of us actually believes in. That's what irritates me the most. That an intellectual pip-squeak like yourself, who stands for absolutely nothing, would have the audacity to come here, into my marvelous den of iniquity, and attempt to save my everlasting soul. At least, the stupid curé believed in something. At least, he was capable of being frightened off by the slut's nakedness. But not you. Not the likes of you!"

The man's bitterness in no way diminished the impact of what he was saying. I was stunned, and my mind was a mess.

An irrational whirling maelstrom.

Was it true?

Was it possible?

"That old bastard," Raxx continued, "is still trying to redeem the both of us. Don't you see that, you idiot?"

I was incapable of responding.

"Well, thank God *I'm* categorically unredeemable," he said with intentional irony. "Why don't I pop a bullet through your useless brain and take you along with me for the ride down into hell? How'd you like that?"

I was speechless, and, for the first time, truly frightened as well.

He leaned over, picked up his Beretta, and rested it on his lap.

"Now, go away," he said decisively, "and don't come back. If you do, I'll shoot you in the face, and you can die right here on the porch in front of me."

He was dead serious, and I knew it. There was no more idle posturing.

When the pain surged again, he shut his eyes and waited for the comfort of the morphine.

"Go away," he repeated, as he seemed to drift off, into a morphine-induced sleep. His taut face and body relaxed into unconsciousness. He looked as though he was dead.

Maybe he was, but I suspected that he was still alive, if barely.

Alone, standing helplessly over a dying heretic, I had absolutely no idea what I should do. I needed to think. I was certain about that, but even the unconscious presence of a man like Raxx inhibited my thoughts, compounding my confusions. Finally, as I'd done so often in my life, I turned to the sea.

I stepped down the steps of the wooden porch to the broad deserted beach and headed towards the Mediterranean. The twilight was beginning to fall, and the blue waves were darkening. In the distance, the sun was ever-so-slowly sinking behind some clouds in the west, in a final, rather astonishing, pinkish-burst of sunlight. It was very beautiful. Perfect, in fact. Who could possibly believe that within such a majestic place, such malediction and depravity would thrive and propagate?

Worn-out from my travels, worn-out from my exhausting encounter with Raxx, I walked down to the Mediterranean, close to the water, and sat down on the sand. As always, I felt an instantaneous comfort being close to the sea, near the chaotic actions of the endless waves. Maybe I could sit here for several hours, put everything out of my mind, and wait for the moon.

But my battered mind refused to vacate itself. No matter how hard I tried. So I attempted to distract myself. For some reason, I thought about baseball, and how much I'd loved playing shortstop in high school, making the tough plays, deep-in-the-hole, firing to first. I'd made second-team all-state two years in a row, mostly because I could hit as well as I could field. But it was always the long throws across the infield that I enjoyed the most, gunning them down at first, making their furious scrambles down the first baseline useless and meaningless. Sending them back to the dugout, frustrated and demoralized.

Then I was startled by Raxx's little bell. Ringing from the back porch. The heretic was still alive, and he was calling for his "whore" for who-knows-what. I didn't want to know. He was, without doubt, the most detestable human being I'd ever encountered in my life, which was saying quite a bit for someone who worked as a reporter, who'd met all kinds of monsters and frauds and criminals. But Raxx was in a class by himself. The truth was, deep in my heart, all I really wanted to do was get away from the man. Escape. Forever. I wanted to get to a phone, arrange for another taxi, and drive far away, as quickly as possible, from this marvelously beautiful place that had become, merely by his presence, something revolting, repulsive, and evil. But I couldn't do it, and I didn't know why. It seemed, for some inexplicable reason, that I needed to see things through. To the very end. I felt, with deep compelling conviction, that I couldn't just get up and walk away, convinced that there was still some unknown, unfinished, yet quite significant business that I needed to attend to.

But what?

I didn't know.

I'd been shocked by Raxx's suggestion that the real reason I'd come to Côte d'Azur was, in some inexplicable way, to "save" the dying heretic. But I knew it wasn't true. I'd only come here looking for answers. I'd come to St-Tropez not only to resolve certain confusions, but to try and fathom the totality of *all* the confusions that had haunted my life ever since Fatima two years ago. So far, of course, my efforts had failed. I'd learned very little today that I didn't already know, and I was now more confused than ever. I was a mess, and I knew it.

As for Raxx, I didn't care at all. At least, I didn't care in the religious context that he'd presumed. I couldn't care less if the supercilious apostate submitted himself to God, but I did, I had to admit to myself, wish that the man would finally, in some tangible way, show some kind of remorse for all the reprehensible things that he'd done in his life.

That he was *still* doing.

Of course, there was a rather vocal part of my inner conscience that was saying, "But why? Why give a damn?" If there's no God, if there's no Church, if there's no heaven, if there's no underlying morality in the world, then why should it matter what some renegade Jesuit does on his deathbed? But it *did* matter somehow, and I knew it. Not because I had any theological interest in the question, but because I felt that it was necessary, for some undefinable reason, for every single human being to finally admit his own failings, to acknowledge his sins. And, for *that* reason, I knew that I'd eventually rise from the beach, return to the back porch, and try to talk to the man one more time. I also knew, without a doubt, that it would be futile. Maybe even rash and dangerous. After all, the man had already threatened me in no uncertain terms, but I knew that I'd go anyway. I felt compelled. I felt a need within myself to try one more time.

Within my jacket pocket, I was carrying the little pieces of the broken crucifix that I'd found on my uncle's deathbed, and I'd brought them with me, hoping to fully comprehend whatever it meant. I wanted to learn *exactly* what Raxx had done that day in Fatima, and what my uncle had done as well. Now it was time to go back to the beachhouse, show the busted-up crucifix to Raxx, and possibly, maybe, learn the truth. Maybe not. But, at least, I could offer the dying heretic one last chance to show some final compunction, some final reservation, some final remorse.

I rose from the beach.

The gun went off.

I was startled and shaken by the sharp crack of the Beretta, and I felt an instant flush of frigid adrenaline surging into my bloodstream, as my heart began to race rapidly, recklessly. I glanced up at the porch, but I couldn't see anything. Maybe the man had killed himself. It seemed to me a terrifying possibility, not only in-and-of-itself, but because the man would have died without any kind of admission, remorse, or repentance.

I quickly rushed up the beach to the house and flew up the back steps to the wooden porch. Raxx was sitting exactly where he'd been before, holding the Beretta in his right hand. He seemed half-dead, staring down impassively at the wooden floor of the porch. The young prostitute was lying, slumped on the floor, in front of him. The tray of food she'd been carrying was scattered all around her, and her red blood was rapidly pooling beneath her. I rushed over, knelt down, and held her helplessly in my arms. There was a bullet hole through her brain. She was dead already. Maybe she'd died instantly, not even fully aware that she was being murdered, but her limp body was still warm, and it was still in the process of shutting itself down. Blood flowed straight down her face from the hole in her forehead in thick streaks of eerily-bright-red. Even more blood was gushing from the back of her head. Desperate, I held the woman close, soaked in her warm blood, just in case she had even-the-slightest-trace of consciousness left within her.

So she wouldn't be all alone.

When I was certain that she was gone, I stared at Raxx who seemed rather amused.

"She was just a whore," he said.

I was astonished. Completely revolted by the man's callousness. But he wouldn't let me get away with it.

"But that's exactly what *you* thought of her, too," he reminded me.

Sadly, once again, the evil man was correct. Earlier, when I'd heard the little bell ringing, when I was still on the beach, I'd thought of the young woman in *exactly* those terms, as a "whore," as nothing else, and I felt ashamed of myself.

Raxx lifted the barrel of the gun to his temple. His hand wavered a bit. Not from irresolution, but from infirmity.

"How'd you like to see this?" he asked.

Malevolently.

I was horrified.

"Don't!"

He was clearly amused. He lowered his weapon and pointed it right at my face.

"How about you?" he asked with condescension. "You're certainly expendable. You're just somebody's stupid nephew. Just somebody's stupid ex-boyfriend. Just another ignorant apostate. Just some fool who wouldn't even know the difference between an infidel, a heretic, a schismatic, or an apostate. Am I right? Fallen-away Catholics like you are a dime-a-dozen. A dime-a-thousand. A dime-a-million."

My fears were complete and reflexive.

With an almost numbing effect.

As if completely paralyzed, I stared intently at the Beretta, listening to the verbal abuse of the man who, as always, seemed so perfectly horrible because he was so often perfectly correct. He seemed to know, as if by instinct, exactly how to expose me to myself. It was extremely painful, fully exacerbating the horror of the death I was facing. Nevertheless, I still refused to submit myself to this malevolent man, to demean myself, regardless of what the man might do.

"Well, what's so special about *you*, Raxx?" I asked. "What have you done that's so noteworthy? You took some quirky nonsense from

Basilides, combined it with the legend of Rennes-le-Château, then connected the dots with an updated Passover Plot. So what?"

He was remarkably controlled in his subsequent outrage, exhaustion, and animus.

He even smiled.

"Yes, you're certainly your uncle's nephew. Now you can join him in the great, blank, hellish nothingness."

I stared at the Beretta, awaiting my death.

"Give me strength," I whispered, without any kind of conscious thought, somewhere in the back of my mind.

The gun went off.

I was blown back to the ground even before I sensed the pain for the first time. Most probably, I'd blacked out, momentarily, but I couldn't be sure, but I was *definitely* hit. I was also in shock, which I realized was a good thing. With tremendous effort, I managed to sit up. The most excruciating pain seemed to be centered in my chest, on the left side. When I looked down, I saw the hole in my windbreaker. It looked as though I'd been hit in the left shoulder. Beneath my clothing, I could feel the warm hot blood streaming down my chest and my stomach. My yellow dress-shirt was drenched in bright-red blood.

Although I'd never been seriously injured before, I once worked at the life-saving station in Ocean City, and I knew a bit about open wounds. I knew that I needed to apply pressure, quickly, or that I'd bleed to death. I picked up a linen napkin that had fallen down with the food tray, slipped it under my shirt, and pressed as hard as I could stand. The pain was exquisite, like nothing I'd ever felt before in my life, but, eventually, the blood flow seemed to dissipate. Then, with difficulty, I managed to extricate myself from the dead body of the young prostitute, and I stood up on the porch in the fading twilight.

Raxx, exactly as before, was lying in his lounge chair with both eyes shut. As if dead. He was still holding the Beretta in his right hand, but it lay limply in his lap. There was, undeniably, a smirk on his face. Carefully, I took the Beretta, dropping it to the floor of the porch. Then I touched the dead man's face. It was cold, as if he'd been dead for hours. There was no response, no reaction of any kind.

"Raxx?" I said. "Wake up!"

There was nothing.

The man was dead.

Numbly, I stumbled inside the house, located the man's bedroom, sat down on his bed, and called the local police. They were very efficient. "On the way." "*Immédiatement*." I glanced around the room. It was fashionably decorated, a bit overdone for a beachhouse. On the walls, there were various secular pictures, including one signed by Picasso that looked like an original. Which I found perfectly appropriate.

It was ugly as hell.

But the oddest thing about the room was the antique crucifix above the head of Raxx's large bed. Why did he bother? Was it yet another sacrilege? Then, as I looked more closely at the murdered figure on the crucifix, I noticed something peculiar. Something rather bizarre. Even though, at first glance, it appeared like any other crucifix, the arms of Christ were clearly different. Instead of being spread-out-and-open, they rose upward, almost vertically, and they were nailed to the cross in that strange position. I'd never seen anything like it before, and I wondered what it meant.

Then I removed the little slip of paper that was tucked behind the crucifix. It was the message from my uncle, exactly where Raxx had said it would be. It was written in English. Consisting of four words.

Hell is eternal cancer.

III.

AFTERMATH

Heaven: *"The dwelling-place (kingdom) of God, wherein reside His angels and His saints, in perfect eternal contentment, witness to the manifest Glory of God."*

Hell: *"The place of never-ending punishment for the damned, be they demons or men."*

Chapter 9

Giardini Vaticani

(Friday, August 2nd)

I was distracted, momentarily, by the melodious bells of St. Peter's. I was waiting in the Vatican Gardens on the left bank of the Tiber, surrounded by colorful blossoms, lively fountains, chirping birds, marble statues, and all kinds of lovely trees and shrubbery. Myrtle, boxwood, laurel, cypress, and pine. It was early afternoon, and I was sitting on a stone bench not far from a replica of the famous grotto at Lourdes, which I'd passed on my way through the gardens, reading the inscription:

"Go drink at the fountain and cleanse yourself."

No wonder so many popes found solace in this idyllic oasis, finding peace and refuge from their endless obligations, not to mention temporary relief from the humid upper floors of the Apostolic Palace. I suppose it might be possible to cleanse oneself within these marvelous gardens, or, at least, find welcome serenity in the soft sunshine, the shaded recesses, and the cobblestone paths. So I took advantage of my temporary respite, sitting here alone and meditative, amid the lush foliage, enveloped in the fragrances of the various blossoms, listening to the countless birds, the murmurs of the fountains, and now, the great bells of the great Basilica.

I was still exhausted, of course, and my wound, although well-bandaged, still hurt like hell, despite the painkillers. But I felt oddly relaxed, for the moment, at least, waiting for the Vicar of Christ on earth.

Two hours earlier, when I landed at Fiumicino, I immediately called the Vatican.

"Tell the Holy Father that the nephew of Fr. Bryce Sinclair wishes to meet with him as soon as possible. I'm certain that he'll want to receive this message immediately."

I'm sure it must have seemed like just another likely story, but the man at the other end of the phone was remarkably polite.

"*Uno momento*," he said, putting me on hold.

Naturally, it took more than "*uno momento*," but the man was back much quicker than I expected.

"Come right away," he said simply.

"I will," I assured him, and that was that.

I'd phoned the most important person on the face of the earth, and I'd been told to "Come right away." Even in my present condition, my terrible weariness, it seemed amazing.

Incredible.

I immediately taxied to the Vatican offices, and this time there was no interrogation by some supercilious Vatican cardinal. Instead, I was taken, without hesitation, by a very pleasant Swiss Guard into the papal gardens and directed to the stone bench where I was now sitting.

"He may be a few moments," the guard warned me with a passable English.

"I'm fine," I assured him, but the man wasn't convinced.

"You don't look very well," he pointed out, with an obvious concern. "Can I get you anything?"

"Nothing, but thank you, I appreciate your kindness."

He nodded politely and left. That was twenty minutes ago, and now Barcelos suddenly appeared, wearing his spotless pontifical whites, walking towards me through Giardini Vaticani.

When I stood up, I was surprised by the sharpness of the pain that instantly shot down the left side of my body, but I tried to conceal my discomfort. This time, I didn't bother to kiss the papal ring. Instead, I spoke immediately, impatiently, even before I was spoken to.

"Raxx is dead."

"I know," he said. He seemed genuinely saddened.

I wondered what else he knew.

"Are *you* all right?" the Portuguese patriarch asked with concern.

"Yes. I'm very tired, but I'm doing all right. The hardest part was getting out of that damned French hospital. They kept me there for thirty-six hours."

"The French can be quite insistent," he agreed.

"I suspect the local gendarmes had something to do with it. They couldn't figure out what I was doing in St-Tropez, and they insisted on questioning me three different times. To be honest, I'm not quite sure what I was doing there either."

The pope nodded meditatively.

When he finally spoke, it was a rather blatant non sequitur.

"When Raxx pointed the gun at your face, did you pray?"

It was an odd question. Barcelos must have read the police report.

"I don't think so," I said, trying to answer honestly, "but I can't remember. If I did, it was purely instinctual."

The pope nodded again, as if he knew more than I did, even though he wasn't there when it happened. Then he changed the subject again, completely.

"So what do you think of this place?"

"It's beautiful. Do you come here often?"

"Twice a day," he explained. "So many popes and saints have sought solace here ever since Boniface began his little herbal garden in the Thirteenth Century. Quite often, when I walk down these winding paths, I think that Leo XIII, Pius X, and Pius XII all walked here before me, and I feel extremely unworthy. Almost ashamed of myself."

"Maybe they felt exactly the same way," I suggested, and the pope clearly appreciated my encouragement.

Then, once again, he changed the topic.

"Did he tell you I was there last week?"

"Raxx?" I asked in amazement. "No, he never mentioned it."

The pope shrugged his shoulders in frustration.

"It was useless, but I tried, and I'm glad that I tried. I'm also glad that you went as well, despite your injury."

It gave us both a lot to think about, so the pope nodded at the bench, and we sat down in the shade. Eventually, I broke the silence. I wanted to get some questions answered.

"Who was he?"

"Gunther Raxx was your uncle's protégé. He was born in Carcassonne, with an upper-class Dutch-Austrian and Languedoc background. The precocity of his brilliance, like that of your uncle, was obvious from early childhood. Obsessed with linguistics, biblical studies, and theology, he became a Jesuit, subsequently studying under your uncle at the Pontifical College right here in Rome. His genius was astounding, but your uncle always worried about his predilection for hyperactive speculation and a rather unhealthy strain of skepticism. Eventually, as Raxx grew more intellectually rebellious, he began associating with the lay theologian Maurice Bruckner who hadn't yet veered into outright heresy, even though he was well on his way. I believe you met that poor man right before his suicide."

"I did."

I was amazed at how much the pope seemed to know.

"Then right after Rome," he continued, "Raxx was sent to Nice for parish work, and everything fell apart. Very quickly. Later, opportunistically, he decided to latch onto my 'rising' star, and he convinced his superiors in the Society to send him to Lisbon."

"Surely, my uncle must have warned you?"

"He did," he remembered, as if ashamed of himself, "but I was at a point in my life when I thought I knew better about such things. After all, I was now the bishop of a very important European capital, and I was feeling quite self-assured and independent. I was instantly attracted by Fr. Raxx's almost brazen intellectuality, and I found myself infected with his modernist social vision. Foolishly, I paid no attention to my dear old friend, and I made the clever Jesuit my closest advisor."

"Did you know that he was publishing heresy under a pen name?"

"I knew that he was publishing avant-guard theological speculations under a pseudonym somewhere," the pope admitted, "but I didn't know which specific books they were. In truth, I never asked because I didn't want to know. I guess I found it rather stimulating, rather *au courant*, to encourage Raxx's out-of-the-box thinking, without, at the same time, fully compromising myself. Which was, of course, an abnegation of my role as a bishop. On both counts. May God forgive me."

"So is that what Fatima was all about?"

"Yes, and amazingly it worked."

"Would it have worked without the sexual scandal?"

"I don't know the answer to that. I wonder about it all the time," he admitted, with genuine uncertainty. "I was greatly shaken at Fatima, watching my dear friend die the way he did, attempting to do the things he was attempting to do. Later that night, when I returned to Lisbon, I resolved to rethink myself, but when the scandal hit the next morning, it obviously diverted my attention. To say the least."

He thought about it a moment.

Then he continued.

"Later that night in Lisbon, after you left my residence, after the effects of the liquor had dissipated, after the self-pity had mitigated, I went to my library and read the life of St. Gerard Majella. I knew *exactly* what I had to do. I knelt down on the floor, and I prayed to Jesus Christ, and I changed my life."

I must admit, I was greatly affected. I believed every word, and I felt tremendous pity for the man, for all he'd suffered.

"You know," I admitted, "when I came to visit you that afternoon in Lisbon, I misjudged you terribly, and I'd like to apologize for it. I thought *you* were the heretic. I thought *you* had written the Bernardi Sorel books."

"I wondered about that at the time," he remembered, "but I was too self-absorbed to care very much. Later, I assumed it was yet another aspect of my penance, my humiliation."

"I hope you can forgive me."

"Of course, young man," he assured me, "but the truth is, I deserved whatever kind of disapprobation I received. I might not have been a heretic in the formal definitional sense, but I'd grown shamefully lax and un-Catholic. Lukewarm. I'd become exactly what I'd so much detested in the earliest years of my priesthood: a political cleric, a clever bureaucrat, a smiling phony full of nothing but diplomacy and compromise. And that kind of compromise, of course, is the work of the demon. I was watering down the faith with all kinds of mundane feel-good generalities, and I was betraying my flock, which is, of course, the greatest sin a priest can commit. On top of that, I was encouraging the likes of Gunther Raxx. I'd become a disgrace, a weak and unholy man, and I thank God for offering me the means to rectify myself, and I thank your uncle, many times every day, for serving as the means of my rehabilitation."

"But Gunther Raxx was unredeemable."

It was obvious that the Summus Pontifex was uncomfortable with the word "unredeemable," but he didn't disagree.

"Your uncle spent over two decades of his life trying to bring that man back to the faith," Barcelos explained. "During his long life of so many triumphs, even miracles, Raxx was his most obvious failure. Even on his deathbed, your uncle was still trying to rattle the Jesuit out of his self-absorption and heterodoxy."

I nodded, thinking to myself that the word "unredeemable" wasn't the wrong word after all.

"He understood the allurements of heresy," Barcelos continued, unclearly.

"Who did?"

"Your uncle," the pope explained. "He knew it well. He knew its attractions. He knew its temptations. He once told me that when he was in the seminary, he had titanic struggles with Subordinationism."

"Obedience?" I asked confusedly.

"No, the specific heresy. The notion that the Son is in some way subordinate to the Father. It's one of the most difficult of all theological conundrums. Even the great Tertullian, the greatest Latin theologian of the pre-Augustine era, who'd written the seminal texts on the Trinity, was a subordinationist. It's quite a reasonable problem, especially given the biblical texts themselves and Christ's obvious reverence for his Father, and His willingness to model humility through paternal homage. Most of the great heresies, in fact, most of which spawned in the East, are all, in one way or another, variants of Subordinationism. Everyone from Arian to the Albigensians to the Unitarians have attacked the divinity of Jesus Christ."

I remembered reading about these things when I was a boy, when I was reading Lawson's great book about the Heresiarchs, which my uncle had given me for my eleventh birthday.

"As a young seminarian, your uncle waged a rather stupendous struggle with himself. Hyper-intellectualism is, of course, a primary breeding ground for heresy, and your uncle was one of the most brilliant men of the last two hundred years. But he fought against it courageously, and he prayed his way through it, and he discovered the truth. Then, unfortunately, he fell in love."

I was stunned.

Incredulous.

"What!" I said stupidly.

"Yes," Barcelos continued, matter-of-factly, "it happened not long after his ordination in Rome, when his superiors, feeling that he needed parish experience, sent him to Nazaré, a lovely coastal town on the Portuguese Atlantic. She was a young local woman who was quite active in parish devotions. I saw her one time. Her name was Maria Carmona, and she was very beautiful. She was also very devout."

"What happened?"

"He fell in love with her, of course," the pope said, with a shrug of his shoulders, "and he wanted to marry her. But for some reason, he took a leave of absence, went to Coimbra for a month, met with Lúcia dos Santos, who was a Sister of the Immaculate Heart, prayed incessantly, and finally made his decision. Then he went back to his bishop, confessed everything, and asked to be transferred. Which he was. Immediately. In the end, he submitted himself, and he transformed himself. He became a perfect servant of Jesus Christ."

"And Maria?"

"On his final afternoon in Nazaré, they sat together in the last pew of the little deserted church, and he told her everything. How he felt about her, and what he intended to do about it. She admitted, just as he'd suspected, that she felt exactly the same way about him, and she similarly agreed that it should go no further, and she approved of his plans. Then they said goodbye. Which I'm sure was extremely difficult. Then your uncle walked out of the church and immediately went back to Coimbra. And that was the end of it. He never went back to Nazaré. Never. But for years, he was racked by guilt, fearing what they might-have-done. Fearing that he might have led his beloved down the path to perdition. But, eventually, in time, it dissipated."

I couldn't resist asking.

"Did anything happen between them?"

"Sexually?" he clarified.

"Yes."

"No."

"Are you certain?"

"I'm certain. We had no secrets back then."

"Did he ever see her again?"

"No."

I thought it over.

Naturally, I was stunned by such a revelation, but the more I thought about it, the more I was amazed that I *should* be amazed. Why shouldn't a young man, priest or not, feel the natural attractions of sex and love?

Even my uncle?

"I tell you all this, Bryce, because he wanted me to tell you," the pope explained, making it perfectly clear.

I nodded again.

I understood.

"So, as you can see, your uncle knew *all* the great temptations. The temptations of intellectual vanity. The temptations of heresy. And the temptations of illicit sexuality. Which were, of course, the very things that destroyed his brilliant student, Gunther Raxx. On the other hand, Fr. Sinclair also understood the *other* temptations. The ones that never attracted him personally. Like laxity. Like doctrinal obfuscation. Like the desire to be everything to everyone, and thus nothing to anyone. Like the subtle abnegation of one's pastoral duties. All of the things to which I was not only prone, but to which, in time, I finally succumbed. But eventually he found a way, as you witnessed yourself, to jar me out of my sinful complacency."

Suddenly, I realized that we weren't alone, startled by the unexpected appearance of the same cardinal that I'd met in front of the Caravaggio in the Pinacoteca two years ago. Without a sound, the man had appeared, as if from nowhere, standing patiently about thirty feet away, down the tree-lined path.

Barcelos looked over and saw the cardinal.

"Excuse me a moment," he said, before rising up and walking over to his cardinal for a brief and private exchange. I seemed to sense concern, then relief, on the face of the Holy Father. Then the cardinal withdrew, as imperceptibly as he'd come.

Barcelos returned to the bench, sitting down exactly where he'd been sitting before.

"He's a tough customer," I pointed out.

The pope laughed.

"Yes, that's true," he agreed, "Cardinal Visconte suffers no fools. Especially me. But he's been a blessing from God. The rock upon which the Roman Church currently rests. I constantly thank God for his help, his generosity. I'd be lost without that man."

I was more than surprised.

"By the way," he added, "he was a very close friend of your uncle's, and he's taken a special interest in you."

"Me?"

"Yes. It might give you some solace to know that Cardinal Visconte prays for you every single night."

I was amazed and momentarily speechless. Finally, I asked about the interruption.

"Is everything all right?"

"Yes, thank God, my sister had an operation this morning in Lisbon, but she's doing well."

Unthinkingly, he lifted his right hand to his pectoral cross, raised his eyes slightly, and whispered some kind of prayer, maybe Latin, maybe Portuguese. I was astonished at how naturally the man did what he was doing, how completely unconcerned he was about whatever the apostate sitting next to him might think.

When it was over, he turned back to me.

"Have you made your peace, young man?"

"No," I said honestly. "I have no peace at all. None."

"Should I speak of submission?"

"Is that all you've got?"

"Yes, it's all I've got," he admitted.

"After two thousand years," I said, with much too much recrimination in my voice, "all you've got to offer the likes of me is submission? That's it?"

"That's it," he assured me, "because it's *everything*."

Naturally I wasn't satisfied, and I didn't respond. I couldn't think of anything pleasant to say.

"Before your uncle died," the pope remembered, "he whispered in my ear, 'Be his confessor.' At the time, I thought he meant Gunter Raxx."

"So now you think he meant me?"

"Yes."

"Well, he also passed me a message. One that was completely bogus. It said, 'Be worthy and Angelina will be your wife,' so I foolishly resolved to be more worthy, and she dumped me for it. Now she's married to someone else."

It was impossible not to sound bitter.

"Maybe it will still come true," the pope suggested, undaunted by the facts, which seemed perfectly ridiculous.

"How?" I asked with obvious sarcasm. "Maybe her husband'll drop dead, and she'll come running back to me?"

"We'll see," he said, unfazed.

"And what am I supposed to do in the meantime?"

I was getting a bit angry.

"Submit yourself," he said firmly.

I didn't say anything because the only response that popped into my head was "bullshit," and even in the midst of my present frustration, I didn't feel it was appropriate to say such a thing to this decent and obviously sincere man in the Vatican Gardens.

In the subsequent silence, the pope took out a small notepad and began writing something on the top page. As he did so, I remembered the small broken crucifix that I was still carrying with me, so I took out the pieces and placed them together on the stone bench. Like a jigsaw puzzle.

"What's this?" I asked.

Barcelos looked down.

He seemed actually spooked by the thing.

"Where did you get that thing?"

"It was lying on my uncle's bed the day that he died. It was under the white sheet. He must have crushed it with his left hand."

"Of course, he did," Barcelos agreed, "with his last ounce of remaining strength. Raxx must have placed it there before you arrived. To torment his dying mentor."

"What *is* it?"

"A condemned crucifix."

I was astonished. I had no idea that something like a crucifix could be condemned.

"It's known as a Jansenist crucifix," Barcelos explained. "It was used in the late Seventeenth Century by the French heretics at Port-Royal."

"What does it mean?"

"It symbolizes that heaven is virtually impossible to achieve, and that only certain excessives, like the Jansenists themselves, are possible candidates for paradise. It repudiates the traditional portrayal of Christ on the cross with his arms extended, open wide, welcoming everyone to come to him and apprehend His mercy. Instead, on this foul thing, his arms are raised vertically, barely open at all. Do you see that?"

"Yes"

"Heaven is certainly difficult to attain, young man. But it's as much a sinful presumption to demean the mercy of God as it is to presume that heaven is easily achievable."

I understood.

Now I also understood what the little boy, Francisco, had meant when he'd seen the crucifix at the deathbed in Fatima:

"He hated those things."

Of course. My uncle would have naturally detested such a sacrilegious object, and Raxx would have thought it quite clever to force it into the old man's hand.

"Can I have it?" the Holy Father asked. "I'd like to burn it as soon as possible."

It was clear that Barcelos had developed a powerful revulsion for heresy.

"Of course," I said.

The pope picked up the pieces, and they vanished from sight.

"I'm afraid I have to go, young man," he said, rising from the bench.

I did the same, but I had a final question.

"What became of Maria Carmona?"

"She married a good man from Nazaré, a fisherman, a man named Carlos Mondego, and they had several children. Even though Maria and your uncle never saw each other again, they corresponded for the rest of their lives. She died a few years before him. She was a remarkable and remarkably pious woman."

"Do you think she would have given in back then?" I wondered. "If my uncle had pursued her more aggressively?"

"I don't know the answer to that," he admitted. "She was a good woman, and I'd like to believe that she would have resisted, that she would have helped your uncle to resist, but we'll never know. Fortunately, as things worked out, God provided her protection."

I nodded in agreement.

"Now, take this," the Holy Father said, holding out the little sheet of paper from his notepad. "It's my phone number."

I took the tiny slip of paper.

"Call me whenever you're ready," he said.

"You're doing this," I asked, "because some dying old man said, 'Be his confessor'?"

"Yes," he agreed without hesitation.

"And what's my role in this whole crazy business?" I wondered out loud. "Aside from ruining my life?"

"I don't know," he admitted, and I believed him. "Maybe we'll find out together."

He thought it over.

"I'd like an account," he decided. "Whenever the time seems right."

Since I had no idea what he was talking about, he clarified.

"A written account."

"Of what?"

"Of whatever's happened in your life since you were sent to Fatima."

I wasn't comfortable with the idea.

"About *me*?"

"Yes, about what you're going through. Where it leads."

I didn't respond.

"Do you still have the recording?"

Naturally, I was astonished that he knew about it, but I suppose I shouldn't have been.

"Yes."

"Include it."

"What for?"

"For the archives."

"What archives?"

"Those relating to your uncle. His gifts. His prophesies. The things yet to come."

"I'm a reporter, not a fantasist."

He laughed.

"Fine, then just report. Whenever the time is right."

I shrugged.

It was preposterous.

He lifted his right hand and placed it gently over my forehead, calling down a blessing from heaven in Latin. As with his earlier prayer, he did it so naturally that I was almost taken aback.

It was over.

"Thank you," I said politely, even though I felt nothing. Absolutely nothing.

"When you go down this path, turn right at the Fatima Fountain, and you'll find your way out of here," he said. "Then go home and get some rest."

When I nodded, the Holy Father walked off into the fading sunlight, down a winding cobblestone path, vanishing into the dark-green lushness of the foliage.

Still standing beside the bench, I watched him go.

Once again, I was all alone.

Again.

Chapter 10

Rennes-le-Château

(Saturday, August 3rd)

I stood in the little church and stared at the Fourteenth Station.

At first, it seemed a rather typical deposition of Christ, a fairly familiar depiction of the final Station in the Way of the Cross: "Jesus is Laid in the Tomb." Two men, clearly Nicodemus and Joseph of Arimathea, are holding the limp and dead body of Jesus Christ. Standing at the feet of the crucified Christ, two women are crying, probably the Virgin Mary and Mary Magdalene. One of them is being comforted by St. John.

And yet, there was something not quite right about *this* particular Fourteenth Station. Something peculiar. High in its upper-left-hand corner, shining above the mountain ridges in the background, was a perfectly full moon, which, of course, was categorically impossible because the Gospels make it perfectly clear that, according to Jewish custom, Jesus had to be placed in the tomb *before* nightfall. As St. Luke explains, "it was the day of the parasceve, and the sabbath drew near," and the Jewish Sabbath always begins at sunset.

So what's that moon doing up there?

Was it possible, as some have contended, that the wealthy apostate curé, Béranger Saunière, had commissioned an artist to depict *not* the deposition in the tomb, but rather the conspirators removing the drugged and still-living, crucified Christ from the tomb? So that he could be revived? So that, having established his church in Palestine, he could then, eventually, leave the holy city of Jerusalem, travel north, travel west, and finally settle in southern France, maybe right here at Rennes-le-Château?

It seemed preposterous, of course. Even in my present weakened condition. Even with the moon sitting in the upper-left-hand corner. Even standing, all alone, in Saunière's own church, the Church of St. Mary Magdalene. Even standing a few feet away from the statue of the Magdalene. Even standing a few more feet away from the frontispiece depiction of Mary Magdalene that Saunière commissioned to be painted beneath his main altar, facing out at his congregation, showing her kneeling in some kind of grotto with her fingers oddly crossed. Even though, earlier this evening, I'd visited Saunière's Magdala Tower and his crumbling Bethany Villa, recalling that more than a few Biblical scholars insisted that Mary Magdalene and Mary of Bethany, the sister of Martha and Lazarus, were one and the same.

Whatever *I* might think, there was no doubt that Béranger Saunière, over a hundred years ago, flush with unaccounted-for wealth, had clearly been devoted, if not obsessed, with the famous Catholic saint whom the world knows as Mary Magdalene.

A wave of exhaustion flooded over me. It was overwhelming, and I leaned back against one of the pews. Obviously, I hadn't listened to the pope. Or, at least, listened to his full intentions. After our conversation in Giardini Vaticani, I *did* "go home and get some rest." But not for long. I got up instead and called the rectory at Rennes-le-Château. A pleasant woman answered in French, who was willing to converse in English.

"I'm planning a visit to Rennes-le-Château, and when I arrive, I'd like to speak to someone about the parish and its history."

"Unfortunately, Fr. Vignon's left for a conference in Lyon."

I assumed Vignon was the pastor.

"How long will he be gone?"

"A week."

I didn't want to wait that long.

"Is there anyone else there?"

"One of the historians is visiting again, but he's leaving on Sunday."

"Who is it?"

"Dr. Kingsley. Colin Kingsley."

I'd never heard of him.

"Tell him I'll be looking for him tomorrow night. My name is Bryce Sinclair."

"I will."

Immediately, I booked the next available flight to Carcassonne scheduled for 9:00 this morning, then I sat up most of the night waiting to leave, sleeping rarely, sleeping fitfully, always uncomfortably.

Early this morning, I put on my favorite Caraceni suit, light-gold in color with its distinctive, curved, welt-pocket at the breast. When I finally checked my look in the mirror, despite my injury, despite my sleeplessness, I still cut a pretty decent-looking figure. But it left me cold. It left me feeling empty.

Which was nothing new since *everything* these days left me cold and empty.

I called my boss at the *Herald*.

"I can't work this weekend, Jack," I said without explanation. "I need a few days off."

"Sure," he said, even though he was short on staff this weekend. Probably because he recognized, instinctively, that something was wrong.

"What's up, Bryce?"

"I was shot in the shoulder by a deranged ex-priest in St-Tropez."

He laughed out loud, never for a moment suspecting that it might be the truth. He didn't even bother to press me for the *real* reason.

In the background, I could hear the *Herald* phone lines ringing loudly and persistently.

"Sure, Bryce," he said. "You take care of yourself and give me a call on Sunday night."

"I will."

We hung up.

After arriving in Carcassonne, I hired a ride twenty miles south to the remote mountaintop town of Rennes-le-Château. For some reason, despite the pleasant weather, the whole trip made me feel sick to my stomach. I wasn't sure if it was the fatigue, or the drive, or the place, or some unpleasant ramification of my still-painful wound. But I suspected that it was the place itself, the whole region, in fact, which seemed to me inexplicably bizarre and peculiar, as if haunted in some way.

As if cursed.

Maybe it was all in my mind. Most probably. The work of Gunther Raxx. The work of Béranger Saunière. But now, finally standing in the Magdalene's church, overcome with exhaustion and pain, I absolutely refused to sit down in the pews. With great effort, I fought against it, as if it was a temptation of some kind. I was revulsed by the place, and I wanted to escape. Deep within my heart, I knew I shouldn't feel that way about a church, especially a Catholic church, but I did, and I couldn't help it.

Gathering my strength, I made my way to the back of the church to the entrance, where I stared into the face of the demon. Asmodeus. The creature was particularly, and quite appropriately, grotesque. Horned and bearded, with ugly, extended, clawlike fingers. It was dark and blackish, with only the whites of its eyes being white. Which was also disgusting and disconcerting. I looked away and left. Why would anyone, let alone a Catholic priest, put such a monstrous thing at the entrance to his church?

Fortunately, outside, the cool evening was brisk and somewhat refreshing. Feeling slightly revived, I paused in the fading twilight and looked at the spectacular vistas that stretched out before me. Rennes-le-Château sat on top of one of the five peaks in the region that supposedly formed a rather rare and sinister yet "natural" pentangle. The area was full of mountains and hills and ridges and forests, with numerous abandoned towers and ruins and forgotten old fortresses and castles. Below in the valley, I could see the small town of Espéraza, and not far off, the town of Couiza. This was the region of the upper Aude River known locally as the Razès.

It was also Cathar country.

It was the one-time heretical heartland of the Albigensians, and Rennes-le-Château loomed over everything.

Having seen what I wanted to see, I walked down the road toward a small outdoor café where Kingsley was apparently having dinner. As I rounded a curve in the road, I spotted a shabbily dressed figure sitting on a low stone wall. The man, probably in his thirties, was self-distracted, visibly shuddering in the chill of the falling dusk. I hesitated and stared at the man, but the trembling vagrant never bothered to look in my direction. He was filthy. Remarkably filthy. Probably the town drunk. Maybe the town idiot. I pitied the man, of course, but I couldn't speak French, and I had no idea what I could possibly say, or do.

I just kept walking.

When I arrived at the café, which was nothing more than a couple of outside tables, the place was deserted, except for an older man, maybe sixty, sitting alone at a tiny table staring at a typescript of some kind. He was a largish man, with a full shock of white hair. He seemed perfectly relaxed, and he had a British look about him. I recognized him immediately. It was Colin Kingsley, who'd written a popular book about Rennes-le-Château. I knew about Kingsley's book because I'd just thumbed through it about an hour ago in a little bookstore near Magdala Tower. His photograph was on the back of the book.

When I walked over to his table, he glanced up from his manuscript, and I didn't waste any time.

"I'm Bryce Sinclair, and I knew Bernardi Sorel."

He was definitely intrigued, as well as pleased, and more than willing to have some company.

"I'd always assumed it was a pen name," he said with a smile, with a clipped English accent.

"It was," I assured him.

He nodded at an empty chair.

"Have a seat. Please."

Wearily, I sat down at the small table.

"Thank you."

"Would you like something to eat or drink?" he asked. "You look a bit worn-out."

"No, I'm fine. Just a bit tired."

He nodded, looking at me with curiosity.

"Can you tell me who Sorel really was?"

"His name was Gunther Raxx. A heretical Jesuit who died two days ago in St-Tropez."

"I see," he said, but I had no idea what he imagined that he could "see."

"We weren't friends," I confided, hoping to put Kingsley at ease.

"He was quite imaginative," Kingsley admitted, "there's no denying it. But he was also a bit of an intellectual sensationalist, wasn't he? I don't believe he had a serious interest in Rennes-le-Château. Actually, I don't think he had any interest in the truth at all."

"Why would you say that?"

"I think it was perfectly clear that he was simply using the story of this place to attack and undermine the church. Which, of course, is patently dishonest."

"Tell me more."

"Well, let's face it, young man, there's not a shred of evidence for any of this Christ-came-to-France stuff. Henry Lincoln got it from some anonymous Anglican minister who'd heard 'second-hand' that Saunière had discovered 'incontrovertible proof' that Christ had survived the crucifixion. What a load of nonsense! To be honest, for those of us who take the mystery of this place quite seriously, the expression 'incontrovertible proof' is always good for a laugh. It's like aliens and fourth dimensions and the Philosopher's Stone!"

Kingsley obviously found such things quite amusing, and he took a moment to enhance his pleasure with a stiff drink of what looked like warm German beer. Then, having aroused my interest, the gregarious Brit picked up right where he left off.

"After all, what would possibly constitute 'incontrovertible proof' anyway? A skeleton? A mummified body? A tomb? Some stupid document? Some ingenious cipher? Some pictograms? Any of which, of course, could have been fabricated, thus easily refuted."

He was enjoying himself, and I didn't mind at all. I assumed that Kingsley had sounded off about all this stuff in his past, countless times perhaps, and that he still enjoyed every single minute of it.

"After all, how could Saunière, some insignificant, little country priest, have blackmailed the monolithic Catholic Church!"

He scoffed.

"Even if he did have some kind of unsettling document in his possession, why would the Vatican, if it was so totally deceptive and evil, not simply eradicate the little French pest? Back in 1209, they marched into this region under Simon de Montfort and slaughtered thousands of Cathars to obliterate the Albigensian heresy. Why would they hesitate to shut up some pipsqueak prelate?"

I couldn't disagree.

"Besides, the whole Passover Plot business is awfully thin. Awfully old hat. It's just a modern revival of a rather common attack used against the church way back in its earliest days: deny the crucifixion, deny the death, then you can deny the Resurrection. Then the whole edifice of the Catholic Church, and *all* Christianity for that matter, comes tumbling down. Basilides claimed it. So did the fourth Sürah. So did the Cathars. It's ridiculous, of course. People can legitimately argue all they want about the Resurrection, but no serious historian would ever deny the fact that a man named Jesus Christ was crucified on Golgotha under the orders of Pontius Pilate. Or that he died in Palestine. Or that there's not a single historical reference to Jesus Christ after 33 A.D. Or in any other location but Palestine."

"What about Magdalene?"

"What about her?" he responded good-naturedly. "It's another totally bogus issue. There's no insinuation anywhere, in the Bible or anywhere else, that she was the lover of Jesus Christ. It's not even clear *who* she was. Was she Mary of Bethany, the sister of Martha? Was she Mary Clopas? Was she 'the woman taken in adultery'? Or was she just another of the many disciples, a supportive friend of Christ's mother, whom we know today as Mary Magdalene? Maybe she was a combination of some, or maybe even all, of those fascinating women? Scholars have no idea, and it's as dishonest to sexually associate her with Christ, as it would be to assume that any of the other women mentioned in the Gospels had been his lover. Like Martha for example. Or Susanna. Or why not Joanna?"

The animated Englishman leaned over the table, winked, and took another hit at his warm dark beer.

"Are you Catholic?" I asked.

"I'm not."

"Christian?"

"I'm agnostic."

He seemed perfectly satisfied with the idea.

He continued.

"But I do my best to be an honest one. I know quite a lot about Rennes-le-Château, and I know a few things about the history of this world, but, after all, how could I possibly know about God, or gods, or miracles, or any of the rest of it? How could I possibly know?"

I didn't comment. I knew the man's point of view all too well. Backwards and forwards. So I turned the conversation back to Rennes-le-Château.

"Where do you think Saunière got his money?" I asked.

"It's in my book!" he kidded. "Surely, you've read it?"

I smiled.

"If you tell me now," I assured my new friend, "I'll buy your book later tonight."

"You promise?" he asked, rather childishly.

"I promise," I promised. "So where did the money come from?"

"Grave robbing," the Englishman answered, almost offhandedly, as if it was obvious. "The Visigoths amassed enormous treasures which they brought into this area and which were never fully accounted for. It was their traditional habit to bury their royalty with gold, and I'm convinced that Saunière uncovered a few such tombs in the area, and given what Marie Denarnaud told Noel Corbu, I assume there's still more of it hidden somewhere in the region. Whether it was Caesar's gold, or Herod's gold, or Solomon's gold, I have no idea. Maybe someday, when more is discovered, we'll figure it out."

I thought it over. I thought how extraordinary Kingsley's solution to the Saunière mystery really was. Buried gold, ancient Visigoth treasure, all the stuff that dreams are made of, and, yet, how banal it seemed when compared with Raxx's Christ-Simon-of-Cyrene-Merovingian scenario.

Raxx was right, in a way, and it's hardly surprising that he stayed within the Catholic Church even after he'd lost his faith, because without Christ and the church everything else in this incredible world seemed perfectly petty and ordinary.

Banal.

Kingsley knocked off his beer, thumped the empty bottle down on the table, and looked at me with another smile.

"I suspect, as usual, I've been talking too much."

"Yes, you have," I agreed, "but I've enjoyed it very much."

A young woman suddenly appeared from inside the café, approaching the table.

"Let me buy you a beer?" the gregarious Englishman insisted.

"Thanks," I said, "but not tonight."

By now, the young woman, who was maybe a waitress, maybe not, was standing beside our table.

She was very attractive.

"There's a call for you," she said to Kingsley, with a charmingly-Frencified English.

The Brit nodded, smiled at me, and left the table. The phone was obviously inside the café somewhere, so I was left alone with the young woman. She sat down in Kingsley's chair and looked directly into my eyes. She had short dark hair, dark pretty eyes, purple eyeliner, and a mysteriously confident smile.

"Are you together?" I asked, wondering if, in some way, she was associated with Kingsley.

"No," she said dismissively, "but he's a likeable old fool."

Which seemed a bit harsh, but maybe she didn't mean it to sound as bad as it sounded.

"I'm meeting some friends later tonight," she said, "why don't you come along?"

Even though nothing explicit was said, I felt certain that it was some kind of sexual proposition, but not the kind that involved money.

She reached out her hand and placed it over mine. Her touch was warm and gentle. Seductive. I realized that I hadn't been touched by a woman in two years. Two years exactly. On her wrist, even in the dark, I could see a small amulet on her silver bracelet with the word "Abrasax" spelled out. Exactly as the Basilidians had marked themselves eighteen centuries ago.

"It's kind of a party," she said. "When the moon is full, we like to celebrate with Aphrodite in a secluded clearing not far from here."

She assumed that I knew what she meant, and she was right. She was referring to something called the Convocation of Venus, an explicitly sexual and black-magic ritual that Béranger Saunière had taken part in over a hundred years ago, and that Gunther Raxx, more recently, had taken part in as well.

As for me, I had to admit that I was powerfully attracted by the young woman's warmth, her interest, her seduction, her lust, and her complete lack of inhibition.

"I'm Catholic," I lied.

"No, you're not," she said, as if she knew, without a doubt, that I was lying. "You're just like me, unattached, wanting more, and lonely."

She seemed remarkably beautiful in the moonlight. Her darkish eyes were animate with lust and rebellion. But there was also a simultaneous and contradictory deadness lurking within those same eyes, as if she'd been imprisoned somehow, trapped within some kind of demeaning labyrinth of her own making, as if her total freedom had become a kind of slavery.

She stood up abruptly, bent over, and kissed my mouth. I was taken by surprise, and I didn't resist. Her mouth was moist, and her taste was astonishingly sweet and alluring. When she pulled away, I wanted more.

"Meet me here at 11:30," she whispered.

I looked up. At her loveliness. She was braless, in a tight black t-shirt. In tight black jeans. She seemed exhilarant with raw sexuality.

She smiled.

"It'll change your life forever."

I had no doubt.

She turned around and walked away, and I watched her go, watching every single seductive movement.

Chapter 11

Toulouse

(Saturday, August 3rd)

I was now wandering the streets of Toulouse.

I'd arrived at Gare Matabiau just before midnight, booked a three-a.m. redeye back to Rome, and had some time to kill. I'd been advised about several places of interest by one of the train porters, but I wasn't looking for anything in particular. I was actually feeling a bit better physically, certainly better than I'd felt in Rennes-le-Château. My overall exhaustion had somehow leveled out. Into a mild, yet not uncomfortable numbness. I didn't know why I was feeling better, but I was grateful.

Even at night, Toulouse was perfectly lovely, with canals, mansions, and its forty-nine towers. The ancient city was world-renowned as *la ville rose*, but, at night, of course, I couldn't see the city's famous reddish hues. Or the various rose-colored tints of many of its buildings. But I could, nevertheless, sense its pleasant ambiance, its ebullience. The people of Toulouse, the capital of the entire Midi-Pyrénées region, were reputed to be the most friendly in all of France, to which, of course, a cynic, especially one from America, might have said, "Well, that's not saying very much." But I believed it. Several reliable Roman friends had assured me that the city of Toulouse, the artistic and cultural center of southern France, was not at all like self-absorbed Paris.

Yet it was still the heart of Cathar country.

The over-tolerant Counts of Toulouse, the lords of the great Raymond feudal dynasty, had been excessively accommodating when it came to Catholic heresy. Especially the Albigensian strain. The ensuing conflict with Rome and the northern French nobles climaxed in 1208 when a papal envoy was brutally murdered by a vassal of the Count of Toulouse. An impasse had been reached, and, reluctantly, Innocent III abandoned his previous efforts at reconversion and called for a crusade, and a long war of conquest began. Toulouse finally fell in 1215, and the citadel of Montségur fell in 1245, but the persistent Catharian heresy still lingered in the Languedoc region for over a century, finally vanishing around 1321. At least, *seeming* to vanish, since all of the more interesting heresies always managed to revive themselves eventually. In one form or another.

Yet, despite its uneasy past, I felt perfectly comfortable in the elegant city tonight. All of that had happened a long time ago, and the people had subsequently prospered. They were now renowned for their cheerfulness, much admired for their aerospace industry, and they were still, amazingly, Catholic. Or, at least, what passes for "Catholic" in modern-day France. Besides, the city had no real connection with Béranger Saunière, or Gunther Raxx, or the pretty young satanist with the Abrasax amulet on her wrist.

After arriving, I walked westward from the train station, heading toward the city's most famous landmark, Basilique St-Serin, apparently named for the city's first bishop, who'd been brutally martyred in the Third Century. The basilica, once part of a Benedictine Abbey, was the largest Romanesque cathedral in Christendom, and, in the distant past, it was visited by countless European pilgrims on their way to Santiago de Compostela. Given that it was almost midnight, I wasn't able to visit the interior of the church, but the exterior, even in the darkness, was magnificent, with its striking eight-sided tower starkly silhouetted in the moonlight.

I drifted south, towards the city's vast central square, Place du Capitole, with its inlaid twelve-pointed La Croix Occitane. There were still some people milling about the plaza, mostly young university students. The atmosphere was pleasant, congenial, even vibrant, but I was an outsider, with too many things on my mind, so I passed through the square and headed for the river.

It was now after midnight.

She'd be naked by now, doing whatever she intended to do. Somewhere in a clearing. In the forest at Rennes-le-Château. Even though I was repulsed by the idea, I was also, I have to admit, attracted by thoughts of that erotic young girl who'd tried to seduce me earlier in the evening. Especially by thoughts of her provocative shamelessness. So I did my best, with concentrated effort, to force her out of my mind. Just as I'd done several hours ago, after she'd propositioned me at Kingsley's table, kissed my mouth, and walked away. Somehow, I collected myself, stood up from the table, walked to the Magdala bookstore, and called for a taxi. While waiting for my ride,

I purchased, as promised, the Englishman's book, *The Truth About Rennes-le-Château.*

Then I walked down the winding road and found the vagrant man again, who was still sitting on the low stone wall, who was still shaking helplessly in the coolness of the night. As before, the man didn't bother to look up at me. Once again, I felt helpless and useless. Then, without much thought, I took off my suit jacket and placed it over the man's shoulders. It wasn't much, but it was something.

Later, after an unpleasant drive to Carcassonne, I caught a late train northwest to Toulouse, where I picked up a cheap windbreaker at the train station.

Raxx, of course, had been right about quite a few things, especially my personal failings, especially my intellectual laziness, but he was wrong to assume that the grandnephew of Fr. Bryce Sinclair didn't know a few things about heretics. On the contrary, I knew quite well, for instance, that St. John had referred to them as the "antichrist," that Timothy had called them "ravening wolves" and "dogs," that Tertullian had called them "rats," and that St. Jerome had called them "vipers" and "scorpions." I also knew that Ignatius of Antioch had compared them to poisonous plants, and I knew that fascinating Origen, being the most accurate and most poetic, had compared them to the alluring lights that pirates would place on cliffs over dangerous reefs to lure misguided ships to their destruction.

I also knew, despite what Raxx believed, all of the distinguishing definitions: the *believer* of course, accepted the entire deposit of faith; the *infidel* rejected it; the *apostate* abandoned it; the *schismatic* cut himself off from Rome; and the *heretic* rejected a significant part or parts of the totality of the doctrine, doing so willfully, or as Augustine had once described it, "contumaciously." The heretic remains perfectly obstinate in his adhesion to some kind of heterodoxy.

So *what* was Raxx?

He wasn't a formal heretic in the sense of someone like Pelagius, or even Arius, both of whom tried to maintain their heterodoxies *within* the doctrinal corpus of the church, within the Body of Christ. As Ignatius of Antioch had specified, "Heretics mingle poison with Jesus Christ, just as men might administer a deadly drug within their sweet wine, and thus drink their own death."

Raxx also wasn't a schismatic heretic in the sense of Basilides or the Cathar Constantine of Samosata, because Raxx actually transcended those other vipers, those other scorpions. He was, in a way, a kind of supreme heretic, a most modernist heretic, one who rejected every single individual delineation of the Catholic-Christian creed, yet, surreptitiously, still lurked within the confines of the church, outwardly conforming himself to her visible forms and rituals, while attempting, incessantly, to devastate her from within. He was, for the lack of a better term, an apostate heretic.

What was I?

Most people who know me would have said, "Oh, he's just a lapsed Catholic," just a "typical fallen-away-Catholic." Which was precisely true, except that there can never be any "just" about it. People can call it what they want to call it, but I'd become an apostate, plain and simple, and I was fully aware of the fact, most painfully during the past two years. I was also fully cognizant of the fact that, in the eyes of the church, apostasy is an even more grievous and egregious condition than that of the formal heretic. The heretic, as Chesterton once explained, "is a man who loves *his* truth more than truth itself." But the apostate chooses to reject the full, whole, entire truth, thus violating the innate fundamental stricture of the natural law that every human being is fully obligated to seek out his God, his Creator.

But, as for me, I'd chosen, willfully, to turn myself away. I'd become lukewarm in a way that the good Barcelos could never fathom. I'd descended into a mushy foundationless humanism, a self-serving laxity. The great Catholic convert John Dryden once wrote in *The Hind and the Panther*:

> *Have not all heretics the same pretense,*
> *to plead the Scriptures in their own defense?*

But the English poet might just have easily substituted the noun "apostates" for "heretics," and the verb "ignore" for "plead."

Thinking about such things, as I wandered the silent streets of Toulouse, was particularly unpleasant, but it did, nevertheless, allow me to keep my mind distracted from more incendiary thoughts about the pretty satanist, and whatever she might be doing at the moment in Rennes-le-Château.

A few blocks from Place du Capitole, I stumbled, unexpectedly, upon an extraordinary gothic cathedral. It was stern and stark and perfectly magnificent. Immediately, I felt myself oddly attracted to the place, and I wondered why. It seemed as though the cathedral was partially lit from inside, and, as I drew closer, I thought I heard the faint sounds of music, which seemed absurd since it was now after midnight. Nevertheless, for some inexplicable reason, I walked to the cathedral's front doors, pulled one of the bronze handles, and the door opened with ease. As if by itself. Now I could hear the music quite clearly. It was a choir of some kind.

Within the vestibule, I looked through the tourist information sheets and found one printed in English. I was apparently standing within Eglise des Jacobins. I immediately entered the church and was astonished by its lively, almost flamboyant interior. Behind me, in the choir loft, a rather intense young man was leading a group of singers, about thirty people or so, through a late-night rehearsal of some kind. The voices were lovely, buoyant, even heavenly. At the moment, they were singing a French version of "Holy God, We Praise Thy Name," which I remembered from my youth in Maryland. No one in the loft above me seemed concerned by my sudden appearance in the nave of the church. Most probably, they assumed that I was someone else's friend, or escort, or ride home.

Unthinkingly, I walked down the center aisle and took a seat on the north side of the cathedral not far from the altar. The altar itself was the least-pleasing aspect of the magnificent old church, being a rather modern-and-grayish affair. But the cathedral's interior columns, which rose above and around me, were truly extraordinary. Curious, I opened my little pamphlet and quickly learned that they were quite famous, known as "Palmiers des Jacobins" for their gracefully palm-tree vaulting.

As I sat back in my pew, I read over the short history of the church. I was amazed. It was the first monastery built by St. Dominic and his Dominicans, the religious order which the great saint, armed with the

Rosary, had specifically created to combat the heresy of the Cathars. It was also the order's mother church, its masterpiece, and, astonishingly, it contained the remains of the awesome Dominican saint and theologian, St. Thomas Aquinas, whom many, including my uncle, believed to be the most brilliant man who ever lived. As a child, I'd read a short biography of the saint, the author of the *Summa*, and what I remembered the most was not the man's prodigious genius, although that was perfectly obvious, but rather his staggering humility. The saint always demeaned his intellectual achievements, once referring to them as "so much straw."

I remembered, quite clearly, the amazing incident of the "talking" Christ, which had a powerful effect on me when I was still a child. Somewhere in Naples, near the end of Aquinas's life, the saint was devoutly praying before a crucifix when the figure of the dying Christ spoke to him, saying, "Well hast thou written concerning me, Thomas. What shall I give thee as a reward?" To which the great saint gave the exact, correct, and perfect answer, which astonished me as a child, and which still does, "Naught save thyself, O Lord."

I'd always assumed, of course, that Thomas, who'd been born in Roccasecca, southwest of Rome, and who'd died in Fossanuova in 1274, northwest of Naples, had been buried in Italy somewhere. But I was wrong. The great saint was buried right here in France! Right here in the heart of Cathar country!

How remarkable it seemed that I'd stumbled into this beautiful place, full of heavenly music, bearing the remains of the kind and humble saint. I felt an inexpressible comfort sitting so close to the sacred relics of the holy theologian, and I wished, rather foolishly, that the great Christ on the crucifix over the altar would speak to me as well. Nevertheless, as always, there was nothing but silence. I knew, of course, that it was totally preposterous, even presumptuous, to wish for such a thing. Thomas had been blessed with that kind of miracle because Christ had decided that the scholar-saint had, in some way, merited such a blessing. Whereas, of course, I'd merited nothing.

Nothing but silence.

Eventually, feeling lost once again, I rose from my pew, stared at the altar, and wondered if I should whisper in my heart, "Help me," calling out to the great saint. But I didn't. Quietly, unobtrusively, I left the cathedral, walked to the lovely Garonne River and crossed the gently floodlit Pont Neuf. Halfway across the bridge, I passed two young lovers, holding each other in the romantic moonlight, completely unaware of me, or of anyone else in the entire wide world.

I began to meander to the west, soon losing my way, but, for some reason, I was unconcerned. I had no interest in the time, or my flight back to Rome, or anything else. Eventually, I came upon a huge cemetery that stretched as far as I could see, far into the night, which, in a visually-pleasingly way, integrated the ancient dead with the more recently dead. Not bothering to think about what I was doing, I entered the gateway. I felt quite comfortable walking amongst the dead, amid their little monuments, tombstones, and all the lovely Catholic statuary, all of which seemed to glow pleasantly in the moonlight.

Eventually, I passed a little grotto constructed in homage to the apparitions at Lourdes, with the Immaculate Conception standing magnificently before the kneeling and praying young Bernadette. It was hardly as elaborate as the re-creation in the Giardini Vaticani, but it was still very beautiful, and I stopped for a while before eventually continuing on my random way to I-knew-not-where.

Or what.

Several times, I wondered if I was actually looking for something, but since I didn't know the answer to my own question, I just kept walking, occasionally stopping to read a tombstone inscription, or stopping to admire a marble angel, or a statue of Christ. Then, unexpectedly, I came upon a second replication. This time it was the apparitions at Fatima. Once again, the "Lady in White" stood majestically before the world, this time in front of the three kneeling shepherd children. It was remarkable and powerful. I felt strangely comforted standing there all alone in the night. Maybe it was because it reminded me so much of a similar representation that I'd seen thousands of times in my childhood. It was on display on the side lawn of my Catholic church in Ocean City, and I'd always found it fascinating. Amazed by what it seemed to represent, that God had intervened into the physical world through his mother, through three, young, and innocent children.

Noticing a marble bench nearby, I stepped over and sat down. Wearily.

Then I stared at Mary's face in the Languedoc moonlight. She was beautiful, serene, motherly, and compassionate. Somehow, in her own lifetime, Mary had managed to transcend her own frail humanity and become exactly what we all crave in our hearts, to become serene, to become content.

An hour or so passed.

Nothing much happened. Then it was over. Somewhere in the midst of that missing time, in the moonlit darkness of southern France, I'd looked up at the Virgin and said, quite simply, *"I will."* That was it. It was over. Because what I had meant by those simple two words, as I was fully aware, was "I will now serve your Son." There'd been no miracle. No manifestation. No intervention. The statue certainly didn't speak to me in the darkness. Mary hadn't said, "Come and serve my Son," but I'd answered anyway. I'd spoken out loud, into the coolness of the night, into the darkness of the night. Finally, at last, I'd submitted himself. After two years in hell, I found a special kind of peace in some unknown graveyard in the heart of Cathar country.

I was surprised by how easy it was. How simple. How gentle. I hadn't been struck from my horse on the way to Damascus; I hadn't seen a cross in the sky with the words, *"In hoc signo vinces"*; I hadn't heard a voice in a Milanese garden chanting, *"Tolle lege, tolle lege."* There'd been nothing dramatic. Nothing at all. But I was fully aware, of course, that there are innumerable pathways to Rome and that maybe great men like Paul and Constantine and Augustine required far more dramatic measures than the likes of me. For whom, in the end, it was really quite simple. A simple act of the will. A simple affirmation. Exactly as the Holy Father had told me in Giardini Vaticani.

A matter of "submission."

I looked up at the moon. She still seemed like a close companion. An old friend. That hadn't changed. Yes, I suppose it's true that the moon is rather small, rather common, and seemingly insignificant. Just one of fifty-seven lunar satellites whirling around our little solar system. And, yes, maybe it's true that many of those other moons are quite a bit larger, but only one, Pluto's Charon, was larger proportionally to the planet it orbited. And *none* of those other fifty-six moons, not even Charon, had a greater impact on the world it endlessly encircled. The silver earth-moon assiduously loved and served its lovely blue planet, the planet of oceans, the planet of God's special little creatures, who watched the gleaming lovely moon every single night, reveling in the nightsky beauty.

I was content.

I was ready to accept whatever I had to accept. To give up whatever I needed to give up. To conform myself completely. From now on, there'd be no more reckless flight from Francis Thompson's ever-pursuing God. The "hound of heaven." There'd be no more resistance. I would, quite simply, *serve*. Never again would I say, as had the demon, "I will not serve." I would now move beyond myself, and I would no longer act like a child. An adolescent. Or whatever I was an hour ago, whatever I'd been my entire life. I would now become a man, putting away "childish things," finally admitting what I've always known in my heart, what the marvelous world around me was revealing at every single moment of my existence: that the world was not some peculiar epiphenomenon, some excrescence of chance, some preposterous product of inexplicable and indifferent mechanical-chemical forces. No. I could now admit to myself the obvious: *That* God had both created and ordained the world. *That* Christ was the Logos who'd come to give us paradise if we're willing to submit and believe, warning, "he that believeth not, shall be condemned," yet also saying, "blessed are they that have not seen, and have believed." *That* everything else on the face of the earth is vanity. *That* everything else is cowardice.

Had I finally given in?

Yes.

And I was fully aware of the fact. For over eight years, I'd put the whole huge thing in abeyance, then, during the past two years, I'd struggled with it endlessly, almost unconsciously, and now I'd finally given in. But there was nothing defeatist about it. Nothing at all. Submission to the truth hardly feels like submission. As promised, it had set me free. Like love. Like falling in love. Like submitting to one's perfect true love. As a consequence, it felt triumphant. Completely. It felt as though I'd finally conquered myself. Faith in the Lord, like its constant companion "Fear of the Lord," had given me wisdom. A simple wisdom, yes, but the truth. The one and only truth.

Did I expect the present contentment to last? Hardly. Not at all. On the contrary, I fully expected my life to become even more difficult. I believe in the old adage that God "gives us what we can handle," and I fully anticipated an avalanche of obstacles, dilemmas, even traumas. But I wasn't concerned at all because unlike the hell of the past two years, my difficulties would now have meaning. Ultimate meaning. And I was fully prepared to do my best, offering in recompense my pains and trials. They would, I knew, become a crucial and fundamental aspect of my continuing submission, and I felt confident, hopeful. The future would be whatever it was supposed to be. Whatever God wanted it to be.

I would now serve Jesus Christ. How extraordinary! I was no longer alone. I would soon be back within Christ's welcoming church, the universal Roman Catholic Church, in communion with billions of other servants of Christ, both living and dead.

Once again, I looked up at the sympathetic face of the Virgin, softly lit in the silvery moonlight. Then I whispered, somewhere within myself, "Yes, I'm small, I'm petty, I'm vain, I'm foolish, but I still offer myself to your Son, my Lord Jesus Christ."

For the first time, I realized that I was kneeling on the ground. I felt at peace, yet mildly euphoric. When the latter sensation passed away, as I knew it would, I felt content. I felt "right."

This is what's meant, I realized with gratitude, by the "resipiscence of the apostate."

Later, when I stood up and sat back on the bench, the sharp shooting-pain in my left shoulder reminded me that some things hadn't changed at all, and I smiled at the reminder. Then I looked at the statues of the three children, kneeling prayerfully before the Blessed Virgin. First, I looked at Lúcia, the oldest, whom my uncle had met and befriended in Coimbra when he was desperately struggling with his illicit passion for Maria Carmona. I wondered what they might have talked about. What my uncle might have said to Lúcia dos Santos of Fatima. After all, what does one say to the most extraordinary person on the face of the earth? What does one say to someone who's spoken with the mother of Christ? Did they talk about the Virgin? Did they talk about the Virgin's prophesies? Did they discuss his problems with Maria? Or maybe even Lúcia's problems, whatever they might have been? Or did they simply talk about the weather? About the Lusitanian sunshine?

I looked at the other two children, Lúcia's beloved cousins, the pious little sister and her little brother, whose imminent deaths the Virgin predicted, who died of agonizing illnesses within two and a half years of the 1917 Miracle of the Sun. Jacinta Marto, the "prayerful" one, whose body was found incorrupt when she was disinterred in 1935. And Francisco Marto, also intensely prayerful, who, like his sister, had moved down the inexorable path toward canonization. I wondered if the little boy that I'd met in Fatima at my uncle's deathbed two years ago had been named for Francisco Marto.

I wouldn't be surprised.

Suddenly, it dawned on me that I'd met the young boy not *just* two years ago, but *exactly* two years ago, given that it was now tomorrow, long after midnight, on the fourth day of August.

Then I realized something else.

I realized *everything*. It happened in a single instantaneous flash of comprehension. I'd been blind, of course, and now I could see.

Was it possible?

Chapter 12

Casa Cabeço

(Sunday, August 4th)

"Over there," I said, directing my taxi driver, pointing to the right of Casa Cabeço monastery where my uncle had spent the last five years of his life.

When the taxi came to a stop, I looked up the stony path to the right of the monastery, and I saw her kneeling in the cemetery, exactly as I'd first seen her two years ago.

I paid the driver, then started up the pathway. I'd managed to get a little sleep on the flight from Toulouse to Lisbon, but not much on the train north to Fatima. Nevertheless, I felt much better than I might have expected. When my train arrived in Leiria about an hour ago, I'd taken the last of my painkillers, and my shoulder was temporarily behaving itself. But I was still aware that I badly needed some rest. I'd been pushing myself for several days, relentlessly, but now, at last, I felt oddly confident that everything would resolve itself right here in Fatima.

As I approached the young woman, I realized that I was mistaken. It was true that she was, once again, kneeling in the small cemetery, but this time she wasn't praying, she was tending to one of the graves and its small white tombstone, not far from the stone statue of St. Dominic. Using her gardening tools and various cleaning implements, she was working in silence. For some reason, I had no doubt that it was the grave of my uncle.

Beneath the heat of the bright afternoon, she was wearing a floppy straw hat to shade her eyes. As I came up behind her, I could see little beads of perspiration on the back of her neck beneath her damp and closely trimmed dark hair. Her baggy work clothes were also damp, as well as dirty. For some reason, I noticed that she was wearing two sets of scapular cords over her shoulders, which seemed rather peculiar.

Even though I tried not to startle her, I did anyway. Surprised, she turned around quickly and looked up at me directly. Instantly, my stupid heart was crushed by her loveliness, her innocence, by everything about her. But there was also a marked wariness, along with a carefully contained excitement, within the young woman's dark, moist, Portuguese eyes, which actually glittered a bit in the reflected sunlight.

"What's your name?" I asked gently, as if it was the most important question I'd ever asked in my life, as if the answer to my question would somehow answer *all* of my questions.

"Angelina."

It sounded like melody.

Like a song.

And it *really* did answer all of my questions.

I was oddly overcome, even lightheaded. I felt a powerful impulse to lean down and kiss her lovely mouth and touch her lovely face, but, of course, I restrained myself.

"Do you know who I am?" I asked.

"Yes," she said simply, with caution. "Father said that you'd be coming back."

I was surprised, even though I knew that, by now, I shouldn't be surprised by anything relating to my uncle.

"When did he say it?"

"He wrote it in a little note," she explained, "that Francisco gave to me after Father's death."

"What did it say?"

"It said, 'He'll come back.'"

"That's it? Just three words?"

"Yes, just three words."

"How did you know it was me?"

She shrugged. It was such a lovely and charming gesture that I wished I could figure out how to make her do it again.

"I just knew," she said.

"Are you glad?"

"I am," she admitted, "but I'm afraid."

"Maybe we're not supposed to be afraid," I suggested.

"Maybe not," she agreed, even though she still was.

Having finished her work at my uncle's grave, she gathered her various tools, placed them in a white wicker basket, and stood up in the sunshine. There was a remarkable yet completely unintentional voluptuousness about her every movement. I tried not to notice, but it was impossible, so I forced it from my mind. I wanted to behave myself, to behave properly in every possible way, even within my thoughts. But my desire for this young woman, not just sexually, was overwhelming. I felt the need to hold her forever. Gently. To protect her. To love her. To help her. Which, of course, was ludicrous and absurd since I didn't even know her.

She nodded at the statue of St. Dominic, closed her eyes, and recited rather unexpectedly:

"Come, O Holy Spirit, fill the hearts of Thy faithful . . . "

I responded reflexively, as if I understood exactly what she was doing.

" . . . and kindle in them the fire of Thy love."

"Send forth Thy spirit . . .," she continued.

"And they shall be created."

"And Thou shalt renew the face of the earth."

She then finished the prayer by herself, praying softly, intently, in the bright sunlight, standing in her baggy work clothes and her floppy straw hat. Then she opened her eyes, and I could see that she was pleased. We'd prayed together, and we'd done so naturally, comfortably. Maybe it was a kind of test, but I didn't care, as long as I'd *passed* the test. Besides, I was more than willing, at any time, to call down the beneficence of the Spirit on the hearts of the faithful, on Angelina, on the both of us.

As a consequence, she seemed more at ease, and she smiled for the first time, which drove me crazy, making me feel entirely irrational. I felt, I know this sounds absurd, inexplicably impelled to kneel down in the grass before her and propose. I knew it was moronic, and I knew

I was being a fool. I also knew that I was still unworthy, that I still had much to accomplish before I could even consider such a thing. But the compulsion was still there, even though I didn't succumb, and I can't deny exactly what I was feeling. In truth, it was quite simple. I wanted to be with this extraordinary young woman for the rest of my life. Of course, I didn't deserve her quite yet, and, of course, I had no way of knowing what *she* was actually thinking about everything. But the fact that my uncle had wanted me to come back to her gave me hope.

Gave me more than hope.

"Father taught me that prayer," she explained, "when I was a little girl."

"He taught it to me, too. When I was a little boy in Maryland in the United States."

"Maybe he'd planned for us to say it together some day," she wondered.

"I wouldn't be surprised."

I had the feeling that I'd be learning a lot more about my uncle that would seem impossible, seem amazing.

"Was Maria Carmona your grandmother?" I asked.

She wasn't surprised by the question.

"Yes, they were very close."

"Did you know that they once fell in love?"

"Yes, she told me about it one time. She said, 'We were in love, but never lovers.'"

It seemed quite sad. To the both of us.

"Their separation was their penance," she explained. "Did you know that they wrote over a thousand letters after he left Nazaré?"

"I knew they corresponded, but not that frequently."

She grew thoughtful, pensive.

"When I was sixteen, when I was acting foolish and frivolous like so many other sixteen-year-olds, my mother gave me the letters one day. She put them on my bed without a single word, and I read them, and they changed my life."

"I'd like to read them sometime."

"You can read them anytime you like," she explained. "They're yours now. Father willed them to you."

I was astonished and grateful.

"Could we read them together?" I asked.

"I'd like that."

Then she remembered something else.

"Did you get Father's picture in the mail?" she wondered. "It was the face of Jesus. A detail from the Hofmann painting."

Although I preferred not to think about it, about what I'd done when I opened the package, I answered honestly.

"Yes, but I wasn't ready for it when it arrived."

She seemed to understand.

"Was it the betrayal in Gethsemane?" I wondered, still trying to remember the entire painting.

"No, it was 'Christ with the Rich Young Ruler.'"

I remembered and nodded. Of course, it was! Which was perfectly appropriate.

Then I turned my thoughts back to Fatima.

"The little boy?" I asked. "Is he here?"

"Yes, he's been waiting for you."

"Is he your brother?"

"Yes. Seven years ago, when our parents died, Father became our legal guardian. Then, five years later, when he was dying, he told Francisco to be patient, that you'd be coming back to be his guardian."

"Submit yourself, another guardian will come."

"I finally understood about that," I explained, "for the first time, early this morning. But now that I'm here, I realize that I have absolutely no idea what I'm supposed to do. I feel completely inadequate."

She was unconcerned.

"God will guide you. So will Father."

She smiled at the idea and continued.

"He's actually a lot like Father," she explained, meaning the boy. "He's very special. He has certain gifts."

I had no doubt.

Then she lifted her hands to her shoulders, carefully removing one of the scapulars from around her neck.

"This is for you," she said.

I wondered if she'd been wearing it for the past two years.

She reached up and placed it over my head. The brown felt patches were still warm with her warmth, still damp with her dampness, and it made me feel extraordinarily close to the one I was destined to return to.

"It'll protect you," she said, "even in the coming tribulations."

I wondered if Angelina knew what those tribulations might be, then I read the Virgin's promise to St. Simon that was sewn on the scapular: "Whosoever dies wearing this Scapular shall not suffer eternal fire."

"Father put it in the envelope with my message," she explained, "so I knew it was for you. I've kept it close to my heart."

"I'll keep it with me forever," I assured her.

"Do you know what it is?" she wondered.

"I do. I remember them from my youth. But I've got quite a bit to re-learn, Angelina."

She understood.

"We have plenty of time," she said, as if unconcerned.

"Can we start tomorrow?"

"Of course."

"Will you take me to the shrine?"

"I'd love to," she said, smiling. "It's a marvelous place!"

I had no doubt that it was. But right now, it was Angelina herself who seemed to me so perfectly, endlessly, wonderfully marvelous.

A priest appeared. He was coming up the path toward us, probably coming from the little cottage where my uncle had lived and died. He was around forty or so, maybe Portuguese, tallish, lean, friendly.

"Father," she said to the priest when he arrived, "this is Bryce Sinclair."

The priest nodded politely, almost affectionately, as if he knew who I was.

"Welcome back," he said. "We've been waiting for you to come. Your cottage is ready."

I was astonished, but I said nothing.

Angelina looked at me, finishing her introductions.

"This is Father Azevedo."

"It's nice to meet you, Father."

He looked directly into my eyes.

"Fear nothing," he said encouragingly. "Petrus walked on water."

Somewhere, in the depths of my mind, I reminded myself, "but only when Peter kept the faith."

I nodded to the kindly priest, who smiled again before continuing down the pathway towards Casa Cabeço. He seemed perfectly content in the hot afternoon sun. He walked along, almost merrily, as I've always imagined St. Francis might have done.

"Father Azevedo's my confessor," Angelina explained. "He's very devout, very kind, but *extremely* demanding."

Smiling at her thoughts of Fr. Azevedo, she bent down and picked up her basket. Then she handed it to me, as naturally as if it had been pre-ordained from the genesis of time itself. That I would, inevitably, enter into her life ready-and-willing to help her with her work, which I was.

Once again, I had a barely resistible urge to kiss her lovely face, her lips, her smile, but I didn't dare. I'd learned to be patient over the past two years, and now I would have to live up to my uncle's deathbed message:

"Be worthy and Angelina will be your wife."

We walked together, side-by-side, down the narrow path near Casa Cabeço, into whatever our life together was about to become.

Finally, I responded to Angelina's previous comment.

"You wouldn't believe who *my* confessor is."
She smiled a knowing smile.

S.D.G.

About the Author

William Baer, author of over forty books, has been the recipient of a Guggenheim Fellowship, a Fulbright (Portugal), a fellowship in fiction from the National Endowment for the Arts, the T.S. Eliot Award, and the Jack Nicholson Screenwriting Award. His various books include *Times Square and Other Stories*; *Advocatus Diaboli*; *Psalter: A Sequence of Catholic Sonnets*; *The Heretic*; *The Dark Knight of Assisi*; *The Gravedigger*; *Classic American Films*; *Luís de Camões: Selected Sonnets* (translations from the Portuguese); the Jack Colt mystery series (*New Jersey Noir*); and the Deirdre mystery series. He is a graduate of Rutgers, NYU, South Carolina, the Johns Hopkins Writing Seminars, and USC Cinema. He was also the founding editor of *The Formalist*, the director of the St. Robert Southwell Summer Workshops, and the film critic and poetry editor at *Crisis*.

His other writings have appeared in a wide range of literary, religious, and/or cultural journals including *The American Scholar, Chronicles, First Things, The Hudson Review, The Kenyon Review, London Magazine, Modern Age, National Review, The New Criterion, Ploughshares, Poetry, Quadrant, The Southern Review, The University Bookman, The Virginia Quarterly Review,* and *The Wanderer*.

He lives happily in a log cabin in northern New Jersey and loves pizza, books, sports, and chocolate.

Also by the Author

Catholic-Themed Novels by William Baer:

Advocatus Diaboli

The Heretic

Jacinta

The Dark Knight of Assisi

Selected Other Novels:

New Jersey Noir

New Jersey Noir: Cape May

New Jersey Noir: Barnegat Light

The Gravedigger

Novel

Murder in Times Square

Murder in Nashville

Annie Oakley Mystery

Mary Pickford Mystery

Central Park

Companion

The Sweet Science

Equinox

Selected Other Books:

Times Square and Other Stories

One-And-Twenty Tales

Psalter: A Sequence of Catholic Sonnets

Formal Salutations: New & Selected Poems

Classic American Films: Conversations with the Screenwriters

Elia Kazan: Interviews

Luís de Camões: Selected Sonnets (translations)

Writing Metrical Poetry

Conversations with Derek Walcott